For Margaret, my favorite hand to hold.

Advance Praise

"Every boy longs for a father's love. And even the toughest emotional chain mail can't hide a recluse from the earnest heart of the searcher. Neither the emotional toll of war, nor the protective instincts of a mother can keep Henry McQuiddy from learning the truth about his missing dad and discovering the bonds they still share.

Master storyteller Patric Peake offers a heart-rending look at a journey of the soul and the bittersweet rewards of not giving up…no matter what."

Patricia Hartman, author of *The Ojai – Pink Moment Promises*, *Yosemite – One Last Golden Summer*, *Secrets of Sandpiper Cove*, *Lonesome Mountain*, and *Lost Lake.*

"Patric Peake takes readers on an exhilarating journey of discovery and adventure through the eyes of his young characters in Chain Mail Man. A lovely coming of age novel!"

Dena Hayess Horton, Ojai Scribes writers' group

"Patric Peake writes with raw sincerity; occurrences painted with emotion that tug at heartstrings, urging the reader to enter his world. He is a storyteller in the original sense, visiting the deeper aspects of humanity through authentic stories from his extraordinary life."

Mandy Jackson-Beverly, author of *A Secret Muse* and *The Legend of Astridr: birth*

"In his writing, Pat gives us "a rich experience and understanding of how the trials and tribulations of life experiences can be the blessings of our learnings." Blessings, which include, "loving, compassion, and joy."

Drs. Ron and Mary Hulnick authors of *Remembering the Light Within* and *Loyalty to Your Soul*

"Patric Peake's stories have the unique gift of unexpectedly worming their way into your heart, leaving you with the glow of goodness in action, and a yearning to follow the example. In praise of a good story (or storyteller), this is hard to excel."

William G. Short, Esq. Law Offices of William G. Short
President of Ojai Valley Morning Toastmasters

"Pat's stories are deeply inspiring and real. They brought out my smiles, opened my heart, and helped me remember the power of kindness and courage."

Stu Semigran, EduCare Foundation, President & Co-Founder

"Pat Peake is a truly spellbinding storyteller. Every time I hear a story, whether autobiographical or fiction, I forget everything else and I am transported into a place where only the heart is seen and heard. I weep, I laugh, and most of all I am profoundly touched and transformed by his insights, as well as his deep understanding and love of people, both young and old."

Kamala Nellen, author of *Coaching For Champions*

CHAIN MAIL MAN

Patric Peake

... not all them war casualties show up on a memorial.
Percy Gray

When you're Henry McQuiddy headed to junior high school in a small Iowa town in 1976, you don't care about all the politics and protests of the Viet Nam war – you just want your dad back from that war. You don't care about Watergate or the surrender of Saigon, or any of that.

You care about all those missing in action, about the wounded stuck in VA hospitals for the rest of their lives, about the guys sleeping in parks in their old army field jackets. You care about the heroes who didn't get a heroes' welcome – like your dad.

CHAPTER 1

HENRY MCQUIDDY

WHEN I PULLED THE folded sheet out of its envelope at the mailboxes, a photograph fell out. I snatched it out of midair. Bent and rough around the edges, I stared at it—at me. *Five years old, hanging upside down, my legs wrapped around Dad's arm like a monkey bar.*

I did an about-face and tromped up the metal steps to our trailer, Number 7, gripping the smudged envelope and picture in one hand while I held the short note in the other and read. The trailer steps clanked under my black canvas tennis shoes like rusty armor in a swordfight. I was ready for battle. Marching across the kitchen, I slipped the envelope with the picture into my back pocket and slammed the note down on the table. "You said he died!"

My mom, Doris McQuiddy, dropped her spatula into

the pan of sizzling hamburgers. The stove flame sputtered yellow. The smell of onion and burger grease filled the room. She stood motionless. Her straight hair streamed down her back like blond corn silk and blended with the light brown shirt of her Sheriff's Department uniform. *There it was.* Her shoulders shuddered.

"Mom?"

She turned and stared at the door. "He did."

"No, he did *not*!" I snatched the letter from the table and shoved it in her face. Part of me couldn't believe how I was acting. I don't treat Mom like this, but something inside of me just wouldn't listen to good sense. I scared myself.

She took the letter, gazed at the words, took a deep breath, and gently returned the paper to the table face down. "He's dead to us."

"What does that mean?"

"He's not coming back."

"He promised. He said, 'no matter what.'" I pointed at his picture on the wall.

"Well, he lied." Mom hissed like air being let out of a tire and slumped into a chair.

"No. *You* lied!" I sat facing her across the little table.

"I told you what's true."

"Bullroar!"

"Watch your mouth, son." She fired her green laser eyes at me, gripping the edge of the table.

"Watch yours, liar!"

Smack.

My cheek burned. My chest burned more. Clenching my teeth, I saw Mom grimace, like she was the one who got slapped.

"Really?" I glared at her, rubbing my cheek.

"How's the head?" Even then she worried about my migraines.

"Fine." But nothing about this was fine.

"The Army called me five years ago and told me his mind was gone." She stared at the note. "They put him in a special ward of a VA hospital where they keep the bodies of soldiers like him. I overheard a nurse calling it a warehouse for vegetables. The man we knew is gone."

"But you told me he died."

"I know you, Henry. You can't let go of things. He's not in there anymore." She nodded at the picture of Dad in his Army dress uniform she kept on the kitchen wall right beside the picture of Mom in her dress uniform for the Sheriff's Department. Both wore sergeant stripes on their arms. Written on the bottom of his picture in permanent marker were the words, *NO MATTER WHAT.* Dad's promise to us to return from Vietnam.

I picked up the note written on lined, yellow paper. "Then who wrote this? Sounds like someone's in there."

Doris and Henry,

Released from the dungeon. Manacles off. My quest begins. My wrists heal slowly. Be wary of everyone.

Salutations,

Lance

Nothing else. I pulled the smudged envelope out of my back pocket. On the front, he had drawn three interlocking hearts. No return address, no stamp. Half of me wondered if this was somebody's idea of a cruel joke. But the other half was sure that this was a real letter from my dad. My burning cheek proved it.

"And what about this?" I handed her the picture.

By then she already had on her on-duty cop face, but I could tell it got to her by the way she twirled a strand of her blond hair with a finger like a little girl. That's how I could tell she was upset about something.

"Yes, that's him."

"Well?"

"Mind if I have this?"

That knocked me off my high horse. Dulled the sharp edge of my blade.

"Okay, but I'm keeping this." I folded the letter into a tight little piece small enough to slip into my green coin purse that used to be Dad's. By the time I stuck it in there, she was out the door.

The next day started at the crack of dawn, the first day of summer vacation in McGrawsland, Iowa, 1976. Glancing at Mom's bedroom door, I grabbed a couple of granola bars and a plastic bottle of orange juice.

I left no note. Why should I? She didn't believe Dad's note. See, I had this part inside me that loaded up on reasons to feel sorry for myself. I called it my *wounded soldier*. Mom's slap gave that part ammunition.

To make things worse, I had this other part, I call it my *drill instructor*, who kept telling me to quit whining, suck it up. I don't know which voice I hated more.

Besides, Mom knew where I was going—same place I always go on the first day of vacation—fishing with Nicky Smithers, ever since we could ride bikes.

I grabbed my fishing pole, checking my reflection in the

kitchen door window. *No bruises.* That *wounded soldier* said, *darn.* But the *drill instructor* said, *good.*

"Hey." Nicky straddled her bike out front. Her fishing pole, with a red and white bobber at the tip, wagged behind her like a tail. A bungee cord held a small Styrofoam cooler with *FAST MART* in red letters fastened to the top of her carrier. Her long, burnt orange hair, pulled back and tied into a ponytail, matched the rust around the rivets of our old trailer.

"Hey back." I had a different reason for why they named it McGrawsland Memorial Trailer Park. Most of our rusty homes already had a couple of wheels in the grave, nothing to do with the park and the memorial across the street.

The tallest flagpole between the Missouri and Mississippi rivers stood in the center of the park with a huge concrete slab at the base and a plaque on the front protected by a Plexiglas shield. It displayed the names of all the Iowa soldiers who had died in all the wars, but mostly, the Vietnam war.

Nicky hiked up her jeans on her right pant leg and latched a rubber band around it to keep the denim away from her bike chain. Her leg was pale as chalk, dotted with a few maverick freckles that made it down there from the herd pasturing on her face above.

"Ready?" She put one foot on a pedal.

I nodded pushing my bike even with hers.

"Set." We gave each other a *you're-dead-meat* stare.

"Go!"

We peeled out.

We zoomed down *don't-blink* Main Street.

As we whizzed by One-Eyed Jack's Hardware, Nicky hollered, "Hey, Terrence!" at the young man who always showed up at a bench there at this early hour, legs crossed and the one on top bouncing up and down showing off his chartreuse tennis shoes.

"Hey, Beautiful!" Terrence hollered as we zoomed away. He was the only living human who could get away with calling Nicky that.

From there we raced full throttle all the way to the gravel causeway, our poles lashing the air behind us. A tractor ahead fed us a cloud of gray dust. The finish line was where the causeway went over the culvert. Our bikes skidded to a stop side-by-side in the gravel. We called it a tie.

The culvert connected McGrawsland Lake to the

backwater marsh across the road, the runoff from the Wapsipinicon River that fed the lake. The marsh soaked dying trees, thick reeds, and tall shrubs in a foot of mucky water. Rare visitors to the place reported deadly water moccasins.

A sudden flurry of wings turned our heads as a huge great blue heron lifted out of the reeds from its fishing spot. That's when I spotted it—a metallic vest, gleaming in the brief moments that the sun reached it through the trees. *Is that a man?*

I elbowed Nicky. "You see that?" I know. I'm not supposed to hit girls, but Nicky was different. She hit back —harder. And she could catch a crappie better than any guy I knew.

"Not so hard, hey." She withheld payback as she peered into the thick woods rubbing her shoulder.

"Sorry."

"Is that a man?"

"See all that shiny stuff all over him?" I asked.

"That's about all you can see."

"Chain mail." I watched Nicky and waited for her to be impressed with my observation.

"What?"

"He's wearing chain mail." She wasn't buying it.

"Right." She studied me with sparkling brown eyes and a twisted smile. Shaking her head, her ponytail swished like a sorrel horse shooing flies. "Like the time you thought that dead elm out in the middle of the lake was a water serpent."

"Shut up. It looked exactly like one."

"Right."

"Look!" The man's eyes gleamed at us. His oversize head had popped up just above a patch of reeds.

"Geez Louise," she said.

Dark hair frazzled out three inches in all directions and covered almost everything on his face except his blue eyes. As he turned away, the sun gleamed off his shiny back. A U.S. Army patch showed on one shoulder. I figured he must wear his old field jacket under the chain mail vest. A vet. The sound of muck sucked at his boots as he marched away, disappearing into dark, green shadows.

"He's on a quest." I squeezed the green coin purse taking it out of my pocket. "Like my dad."

"But your dad is …" Nicky stopped herself.

"Dead?" I pulled out the yellow sheet, unfolded it, and handed it to her.

Nicky's theory was that my dad died in the Vietnam

war, but just was never found. That's why his name wasn't on the memorial under the flagpole. He was *MIA*. She read the note. "Geez Louise!"

"Look at this." I pulled the envelope out of my back pocket. "All these smudges. That man is filthy. They're his."

Nicky nodded her agreement.

"Now. Look at the address." I flipped it over—a sketch of three hearts, linked together. "And Dad did this."

I nodded at the man who'd disappeared into the woods. "He delivered this for Dad—from the warehouse."

"Warehouse?"

"The place they're keeping Dad. Mom told me."

"There goes another marble." She rolled her eyes.

Snatching back the sheet, I stared into the marsh. "I'd like to ask him some questions. He might know something about …"

"Grow up, McQuiddy." Nicky punched my shoulder, this time really hard. "He's a vagrant."

"With chain mail?" I rubbed the spot where there was gonna be a bruise.

"Chain what! Are you completely crazy?!"

"No more than getting a …" This time, I put on the brakes to my words.

Nicky planned to get a tattoo of her mom's name. Her mom died in a car crash four years ago. If she accused me of being crazy, I had a great comeback but rarely used it. Twelve-year-old girls do not get tattoos, not in Iowa, anyway.

"I give up." Nicky fished a lively minnow out of the cooler and ran a hook through its back. "I'm trying the woodpile." She adjusted her bobber for shallow fishing and headed over to a bunch of logs and dead branches jammed against the culvert. She dropped her bobber between two logs.

Sitting on my heels just off the road with my arms around my knees, I stared into the marsh where the man had disappeared. I had a feeling about this guy. Bet he knew my dad in Vietnam. Maybe this guy did deliver Dad's letter to us. Maybe a piece of shrapnel was lodged in Dad's head causing him to lose his memory. Maybe this guy took the same grenade. Maybe he knows where Dad is now.

A warm breeze carried the stink from the marsh, which brought me back to my senses. Still soaked with about a foot of water from the spring rains, the backwater turned into a smelly muck. Marching through that would be tough. Not to mention dealing with the snakes and larger serpents.

I folded the yellow sheet back into a small square, jammed a hand into my right front pocket, and pulled out my green coin purse. The note fit real nicely in there. I slipped the envelope into my back pocket.

"Got him!" Nicky held up a fat silver-scaled crappie.

"Nice," I hollered. "See. Even the fish wear chain mail."

CHAPTER 2

NICKY SMITHERS

FROM THIRD BASE, I spotted McQuiddy leaning against the green hotdog stand beside the bleachers. Propped up on one leg with his eye-burning orange T-shirt, he looked like those plaster flamingos on the rich peoples' lawns in Davenport. Except that he had a shock of brown hair that looked like it had been through a twister. He toasted me with his can of pop, his dark eyebrows rising over his smiling hazel eyes. He knew what I was preparing to do.

"Just lob it in to her, Blanche." Our pitcher, Blanche, was one of those *perfect* girls. You know. Long, blond hair, blue eyes, athletic but feminine body, *perfect.* "Her knees are knocking, and her shoe's untied." I chomped on my gum.

I played third base for the McGrawsland girls softball

team, the Lady Catfish. I hated that name. Only time you can tell when a catfish is a lady's when it's got a belly full of yellow fish eggs. But the enemy had a worse name.

The Westridge Heifers, named for the town's main source of income, rode over in an old white church bus for a late Saturday afternoon game. The heifer was the perfect mascot for their team. That herd sported the biggest twelve-year-old girls I'd ever seen. Three wore lipstick, pale, pinkish, not the red stuff. And the batter? I swear, she must've stuffed a couple of tennis balls under her sports bra. Twelve-and-under, my eye!

The batter scowled at me and pounded her bat on the plate once. I watched Blanche out of the corner of my eye.

Just as Blanche swung her arm back to pitch, I hawked up a big, loud loogy and spat a dark, brown gob onto the baseline. I always chew a whole pack of Black Jack gum. Mixed with my spit, it looked just like the tobacco juice the big leaguers spat, only thicker. One of the benefits of my summer allergies.

I glanced at the dugout and caught Coach Bernstein's glare. I knew why, but pretended not to notice. The spit messed up the baseline pretty bad. The batter, one of the larger heifers, just about peed her pants staring at the gross gob with her mouth open as the ball dropped into the catcher's mitt.

"Strike three!"

"What'd I tell ya!" I ran in with my team to bat. McQuiddy choked on his soda with laughter and about fell over. The boy couldn't walk and pick his nose at the same time cuz he had grown so fast.

I led off, glancing at McQuiddy as I stepped up to the plate. He chomped on some corn chips and washed them down with pop. He had switched to the other leg to prop himself. At least one of those legs had to be hollow, I swear. Always had something in his mouth but skinny as a cane pole.

I'd already knocked one way over the right field fence, so the pitcher was tossing me balls so far outside I'd have to be Plastic Man to get to them. Got one of the original comic books in my collection.

"Hey, Nicky! Check out right field," McQuiddy said, cupping his hands.

"I know. The right fielder has five thumbs." I'm a switch hitter, and I actually hit harder left-handed. I own right field when I bat lefty.

"No. Over the fence."

"No problem." I kissed Annie on her label. Called my bat *Annie Oakley* after that Western markswoman. I pointed her at the right field fence taking aim.

I froze. That so-called Chain Mail Man marched along the Wapsi River out at the end of the soybean field just beyond the right field fence. You could see him on account of the sun gleaming off his metallic vest. I looked back at McQuiddy. "Geez Louise!"

"Strike!" I gave McQuiddy my death scowl.

After the game, we always hang out at the Fast Mart. There's this one spot in the candy section where the owner can't see you when you swipe a Butterfinger. We only did it once, to see if we could. McQuiddy's mom being a cop, we didn't want to press our luck. That's where McQuiddy proved to me he was even crazier than I thought.

"We gotta see if we can find him, Nicky. He may know Sgt. McQuiddy."

"You mean Sgt. McQuiddy as in your dad or Sgt. McQuiddy as in your mom? Because if she knew what you're up to, she'd have your hide." I watched his eyes narrowing like he was looking at something far away. "You're kidding, right?" I noticed his jaws tightening, even though his candy bar was still in its wrapper. "You're *not* kidding. What if this guy's one of those mass murderers who slashes you a thousand times with a broken Coke bottle and chops up your bones? Huh? What then?"

"We stay away. Just tail him. See what he does."

"Sure." I gripped my bat in both hands. "You, me, and Annie Oakley here. You see that shot over the right field fence? They never did find the ball."

Ignoring all my questions, McQuiddy tore the wrapper off his candy bar and tossed it in the trash on the way out of Fast Mart. *Why do I follow this boy?*

Nobody gave me guff anymore about walking with a boy, especially since I carry a bat. The last guy who did got beat up. Not bad. I did just enough to humiliate him, you know, my knees on his arms, my fist six inches from his face.

We turned down a row of the soybean field and marched to where McQuiddy thought he saw the man disappear into the thick patch of reeds along the river bank. The air thickened from the storm-promise made by some billowing orange thunderheads in the distance. They matched the boy's T-shirt. A slight breeze from the river carried the faint memory of cooked meat.

McQuiddy went into his drill sergeant act, inspecting the reeds. I think he let his mom and dad both being sergeants get into his head.

The boy had his quirks. Like this military thing with that army belt on his bike. He marched up and down the reeds looking them over. The tall stalks stood at attention, like thin, seven-foot soldiers, shoulder to shoulder. Their sharp-edged leaves crossed like little swords.

"Here." McQuiddy pointed at a break in the ranks. Stems bent to the ground, leaves crushed. A narrow passage had been trampled deep into the reeds.

"Let's recon." The boy poked his head into the passage, but braced himself to run.

"Yeah, right." I shook my head. *Recon*. Bet it's not even a real word. "See anything?"

"Nah."

"Hear anything?" I tried to whisper.

McQuiddy shushed me with a finger to his mouth. He cocked his head and held his breath.

"No. Nothing. I'm pretty sure he's gone."

"*Pretty* sure?"

"Very sure." McQuiddy took a deep breath, shielded his face with an arm, and stepped into the narrow path.

"Whoa, boy! What're you doing?" I grabbed his arm.

He pulled free. "Investigating."

"It's your head needs investigating." I knew it was hopeless. "I swear McQuiddy, most your marbles have already leaked out of that hole in your brain."

He pressed on ignoring my comment. I pressed Annie Oakley in front of me and, against my better judgment, followed the boy.

The path tromped through the reeds, curved right, then left. The dipping Iowa sun and rising breeze played tricks on me. Slivers of light danced between the leaves creating kaleidoscopic fantasies of movement.

"Awk, awk, awk!" An explosion of fluttering wings and brilliant colors had me jumping out of my skin.

"Pheasant!" McQuiddy shouted in a whisper.

Several times after that, I grabbed McQuiddy's shirt to pause and listen again. It bugged the boy, but big deal.

Then McQuiddy stuck up an arm and froze. "Check it out."

We stopped at the entrance to a clearing. The familiar smell of rich, black loam greeted me, reminding me of countless digs for worms. It was mixed with the faint smell of cooking from the campfire in the center. A ten-foot-diameter circle of freshly exposed soil lay before us where a platoon of reeds had been yanked up by their roots and tossed to the sides.

"This is creepy," I said.

"Check the perimeter." He marched to the center and sniffed the ashes of a campfire. I stepped in and started poking around the edge with my bat.

"Look at this." I took a knee picking up a crushed soda can, flattened into a perfect circle of aluminum stacked on four others. "The pop-top's missing. Look." I held it up above my head so the sunlight could hit it. "There's five of them, all with the tops taken off."

"Now that's a clue." McQuiddy didn't look up.

I set the discs of aluminum back in place. "Okay, McQuiddy. What brilliant observation do *you* have?"

"He cooks his Spam in the can." McQuiddy pointed to the distinct rectangular outline in the ashes of the fire.

"Where's the can?" I joined him at the campfire.

"I guess he took it with him." He took a stick and poked around in the ashes, smiling. "See any body parts?"

I punched him good. "McQuiddy, that's not funny."

"Neither is your fist."

Snap! A branch cracked deep inside the tunnel of reeds.

My fingers latched onto McQuiddy's wrist like a handcuff.

"Geez, Nicky!" He grabbed my fingers and tried to pry them loose. "You just about scared my pants off!"

"Now, there's an image." I glanced at his shiny brass military belt buckle.

Snap! I tightened my handcuff hand another click on his wrist. A different sound—*metallic.* I pointed my quivering bat at the entrance in the reeds. "What's *that* sound?"

"What sound?" Then he heard it. Tinkling—like loose change rattling in your pocket, only a *lot* of loose change.

"That!" I raised Annie Oakley.

A shadow spilled on the floor of the leafy entrance like ink. McQuiddy drew back, dragging me with him, my hand still locked on his wrist.

Huh, huh, huh. We heard breathing like a dog panting from a hard run.

"Get away!" I shouted.

The breathing stopped. The shadow froze. So did we.

"No." A deep voice replied.

The shadow now filled the clearing.

"Whoa!" McQuiddy whispered.

A mass of dark brown hair and camouflage clothing

clogged the only way out like instant vegetation. Except that the vegetation wore a shiny metal vest. Two blue eyes darted back and forth around the edge of the clearing. They stopped at my feet.

I pressed back against the wall of reeds, pulling McQuiddy with me. It wasn't fear that hit me. It was more like hatred. Don't know why. I felt like this momma raccoon McQuiddy and I came upon once defending her two kits. She had stood up on her hind legs and hissed. I remember her eyes gleaming out of that black mask across her face. Those brown little beads said, "I will do *anything* to protect my babies." This man was here not only to hurt *me*, but also my friend and even my family. I let go of McQuiddy so I could grip my bat in two hands.

Henry stepped in front of me. "What d'ya want!"

That shiny metal stuff crinkled on his back as the man raised a camouflage sleeve and pointed with a huge, leathery hand *at me*. "Mine."

"Like heck," McQuiddy said. "She's *my* friend."

"Mine." He pointed at my feet.

We looked down at the five discs of aluminum stacked on the ground.

The man lifted what looked like a broom handle with a

coffee can stuck to the end. *Whump!* He slammed it down leaving an inch-deep, circular crater in the black earth. The can was filled with something solid and heavy. I felt the ground shake from several feet away.

"Mine!" He took a step forward.

I raised my bat over my shoulder. "You wanna play? Okay, I'll play. Come meet Annie Oakley!" McQuiddy put a hand on my shoulder trying to calm me down.

The man froze. His eyes stared at nothing.

McQuiddy's foot crunched metal.

"Is this what you want?" He slowly knelt down, facing the man while his hand shuffled around in the dirt locating the stack of aluminum discs. Slowly, he extended them. The man stared with that glazed look of an animal deciding whether to *run—or—eat you.*

The man's face beaded with sweat, droplets forming on his beard.

No wonder, I thought. The guy must have at least five layers of clothing on his back as well as a dirty, green backpack. A U.S. Army camouflage field jacket displayed a yellow patch with a black horse head on one shoulder and a U.S. Army patch on the other. But here's the weird part. His chest and back were covered with what seemed to be a metal vest. I must admit it did look like chain mail. Maybe Henry was right, but it was hard to tell because the sun had deserted us. It dropped like an egg yolk into a pan this time of day. You could almost hear it sizzle when it hit the river.

The man glanced down at McQuiddy's opened hand and shot out a long arm to snatch the crushed cans. He stuffed them under the flap of his pack, turned away, and started to leave. Thank heavens!

Just as I was fixing to blast McQuiddy for getting us into this mess, the man stopped, turned, and came back. He made a funny noise that sounded like grunting as he crouched at the entrance. *Was he laughing?*

I shouldered my bat, ready to knock his block clear to kingdom come. The boy didn't try stopping me this time.

The man reached into his field jacket pouch and pulled out something. McQuiddy tried to shove in front of me but I shoved back. "Bring it on!" I waggled my bat up and down.

He tossed something at us, underhand. It rolled across the earth—and stopped a few feet from us.

"Grenade!" McQuiddy pushed me away, dived, and covered it with his belly.

"Aaaaaagh!" The Chain Mail Man hit the dirt.

"Nooooo!" I tried to grab McQuiddy's leg.

Ten long seconds ticked in my brain while I waited for us to be blown to smithereens. I clutched McQuiddy's ankle while keeping an eye on the man. He'd smashed his own face into the dirt, elbows out, huge hands muffling his ears.

After several seconds, the man rose to his elbows, trembling. Still on the ground, he started crawling away on his belly, soldier like, using his elbows and knees.

McQuiddy stood. He lifted the *grenade.* It looked more like a mud ball. Wiping some of the black crust off, a white, leather softball appeared.

It took us a full five seconds for our brains to wrap around what had just happened. We stared at the ball. The man stood and marched into the reeds.

"Good riddance," I said.

"Hey!" McQuiddy hollered at the man.

"Shut *up*, McQuiddy!" I glared at him.

The man turned back, facing the boy. The red sunset turned his blue eyes orange.

"Do you know Sgt. Lance McQuiddy?"

The man's eyes narrowed. "Hrrmmph!" He snorted, turned, and strode away. McQuiddy tried to run after him, but the vice grip of my left hand locked on his elbow.

"Sgt. Lance McQuiddy! You know him?" McQuiddy shouted at the dark figure disappearing around the curve in the passage.

"No." Came the reply, and he was gone.

"McQuiddy! Leave it alone."

"No way, Nicky. That guy knows something."

I released McQuiddy's elbow, picked up the softball, and examined it. "This ball met Annie Oakley."

"Huh?"

I turned the scuff mark toward McQuiddy. "I really nailed this one."

The boy just kept staring at the reeds. "He's lying, you know. He knows something."

"What?" I couldn't believe this boy.

"He knows my dad."

"McQuiddy. Have you flipped? What the five-pound fruitcake are you talking about? The guy probably doesn't even know his own name. He's a homeless guy, a bum. When Sheriff Matson finds out he's roaming around here, he'll catch him like a stray dog, put him in a cage, take him to the next county, and release him.

"Well, see here?" McQuiddy pulled out the yellow letter. It says 'dungeon' and 'quest.' And 'trust no one.' This guy trusts no one."

"Geez, McQuiddy! A quest? Really? Only thing he's after is aluminum cans."

"He's wearing chain mail—like a knight. You know."

"Does your mom know about this—this obsession of yours?"

"Mom lied about my dad." He was clenching his teeth again. "I don't care what she says. He's alive, and I'm going to find him."

"So this is all still about your dad?" I watched his face. "Look, McQuiddy, that guy?" I tapped the side of my head. "Nobody home."

The boy just didn't listen. I swear the only time he ever hears me is when I ask him to go fishing or offer him the other half of my Almond Joy.

"So I figure he's like a knight on a quest, like Lancelot and the Holy Grail, only his name's just Lance, my dad's name." McQuiddy folded the yellow note and put it back in his green coin purse.

"Oh my God. The boy's lost it completely." I spoke to the sky. "Not one marble left."

And now there's this guy with chain mail. I give up."

"I don't." The boy jammed his coin purse in his pocket

and marched to the reeds exit.

I threw Annie Oakley over my shoulder, stuffed the muddy softball in my shirt, and followed. I had to remind myself that there's not one other human being alive, besides my dad, who would dive on a live grenade for me. Guess I'm stuck with the boy,

Chapter 3

HENRY

NICKY AND I WEREN'T allowed in each other's homes. My mom and Nicky's dad, Richard Smithers, were about as friendly as two bulls let loose in the same pen. They were always locking horns. Mom's a peace officer for the county sheriff's department and Mr. Smithers was, to use Mom's words, "an ambulance chaser." That's pretty ironic since Mr. Smithers had polio as a kid and, with his limp, couldn't chase a turtle. Actually, he's a paralegal for the ACLU, the American Civil Liberties Union, which Mom's boss, Sheriff Matson, claims is a Communist organization. Nicky says they're just trying to make sure that the common people have rights. I never did figure out who the common people were, but I'm guessing it's us.

Seems Mr. Smithers was on a mission to expose the sheriff's department for "police improprieties," as he called them. Sheriff Matson had a cuff-first-and ask-questions-later policy, especially when it came to what he called "deviants." That would be anyone in town who wasn't a good old Iowa boy or a good old boy's wife or girlfriend. Smithers maintained that the only reason they hired Mom was because they had to. Things got pretty harsh between Nicky's dad and my mom.

Mom thought of herself as one of the good cops. Not like her boss, the sheriff, who hated anything not "clean country living," as he put it. And a woman being a cop didn't fit his idea. Mom got passed up for promotion three times before he finally had to promote her because she aced her sergeant's exam.

I once overheard the good old boys talking about Mom at One-Eyed Jack's. "Like a burr inside my sock," one guy said. "She pulled my dang tractor over, for God's sake. Does she know she lives in Iowa?"

But that wasn't the whole story. Something else seemed to lie between our parents, something like a coiled snake. Nicky and I both sensed it. Something with venom in it.

As near as I could tell, the feud all started between our

parents almost four years ago after Nicky's mom died in that car crash. A couple weeks after that accident, Nicky and I sat on top of a green picnic table at McGrawsland Memorial Park watching her dad pitch horseshoes.

Since the tragedy, Mr. Smithers' face had changed. It hardened, statue-like. He didn't look at people anymore either, except for Nicky. He limped up to the pit glaring at his target. He may have had a bum leg, but the rest of Mr. Smithers was bodybuilder buff.

Along with Nicky's dad, the infamous Duke Doreen and two of his buddies from town pitched shoes, drank beer, and laughed too loud. Duke was known for his ability to turn a friendly conversation into a fight. He volunteered to go to Vietnam and start fights over there, but they refused him on account of his hearing. He wore a gob of not-so-skin-colored plastic in his ear. It gleamed through the long, thin strands of orange hair he let grow to cover it. He bellowed his words like a hog caller.

"Heard they locked him up in the loony bin again!" Duke picked up a blue horseshoe.

Mr. Smithers picked up the two red horseshoes and clanked them together. The muscles in his forearms bulged. "Good riddance."

"Yeah. Good." Duke spotted me and frowned.

I hated him. I didn't know why. Maybe because of the way he looked at me—like I was dog poop on the sidewalk. That's how Duke looked at me right then. I think he was jealous of my dad, maybe because Dad did go to Vietnam and even got a Bronze Star for dragging half his wounded platoon across a river to safety. Duke wanted so bad to fight in that war. Always talking about, *If I was there, I'd have …*

Just then, Mom pulled up in her patrol car and parked in front of Number 7. She spotted me and stepped across the street to the edge of the park.

"Let's go, Henry."

"Mom?"

"What?"

I knew I was on thin ice, but I skated anyway. "Who'd they put in the loony bin?"

She shot a bullet-look at Mr. Smithers. "You happy?"

"You?" Mr. Smithers fired back. The other two guys stood motionless, like they'd just witnessed a fatality. Duke started to grin.

"You hear something funny?" Mom's look drilled a hole right between Duke's eyes and wiped his face clean of any smile. She put her hand on her nightstick and took a step toward him. "Did you?"

"No, ma'am." Duke stared at his own shoes.

Her eyes dropped onto me. "Let's go."

"Aw, Mom!"

"Now."

I trudged alongside her like my feet weighed twenty pounds apiece.

"What's *that* all about?" I stopped, waiting for an answer.

She grabbed my wrist and yanked my arm so hard I felt it for a week and remembered it for life. "Nothing."

I thought life couldn't get much worse than your mom almost yanking your arm off, but it did. The next day Nicky and I went to get kite string at One-Eyed Jack's. Duke Doreen caught me in one of the aisles. Nicky was already out the door.

"You got big ears, kid." He squeezed the back of my neck with one giant hand.

"No, I don't," I said.

"What'd you say?"

"I said, *No, I don't.*"

Duke pulled out his Swiss Army knife, let go of my neck, pulled open the largest blade, grabbed my neck again, and held it six inches from my face. "Yes, you *do*."

I'd never seen my own eyes opened so wide as they were in my reflection on that blade.

"Pretty, isn't it?"

I closed my eyes.

"Wanna feel it?" Cold steel touched the base of my ear. I felt him slide the dull side of the blade up the length of my ear. "Get the point?" Duke said.

Both my ears burned. "Yes."

"What did you say?"

"Yes!"

"Good." Duke laughed like a snorting pig at his own pun.

I didn't laugh. Didn't cry either. In fact, I never told anybody about it. Not even Nicky. I just shoved the door open and never looked back.

"He's acting like an idiot!" Terrence Ashton must have seen the whole deal from the bench outside One-Eyed Jack's.

"Yeah." I noticed myself quivering every so often like a horse trying to shiver off flies.

"Want me to go in there and set him straight?" Terrence put one hand on my shoulder and waved at Nicky across the street.

"Nah." If I was no match for Duke, Terrence was even less so.

We all knew Terrence was a bit strange, but he was harmless. He sat there across the street from the Busy Bea Café watching the truckers drive in from the main highway to get a bite of the best homemade pie in the state of Iowa. I think he was hoping he'd find a new friend. The one close friend he had in McGrawsland moved to Davenport. That was the sheriff's son. Maybe Terrence thought his bright green tennis shoes were some kind of lure that would bring them over to him, like a chartreuse rubber bass-worm brings a fish.

Anyway, it calmed me down to talk to Terrence. At least there was one guy in McGrawsland who wouldn't hurt a honeybee even if it stung him.

CHAPTER 4

NICKY

AS I WATCHED MCQUIDDY and Terrence talking across the street at One-Eyed Jack's that day, I got a real good feeling about the boy. Not many boys would have the gumption to talk to Terrence on account of his so-called "effeminate ways." But Terrence was a good guy. I mean, other than my dad, I think he's the only guy who ever told me I looked pretty in a way that didn't make me feel like a calf being auctioned off at the fair.

He would say, "Girl, you have that natural beauty. Even your ponytail is cute."

"No, I don't, Terrence, not like Blanche."

"Blanche's a cream puff. You're a main dish."

That made me laugh. And the sad thing is, the guy

himself had little to laugh about. His best and only friend, Rocky Matson, the sheriff's son, moved to Davenport a year ago. "People in the big city don't make such a fuss about who you are," Terrence said.

To tell you the truth I didn't get what he meant, but I said, "Why don't you move there?"

"You know why." Terrence just looked at me with those deep brown, serious eyes.

"Your mom." I forgot. "Sorry."

"Yeah, me too. She's had a pretty good run this week. Recognizes me most of the time. When she's all there, she's a real sweetie."

"So are you," I said. "Always."

Four years later, Terrence still sits in front of One-Eyed-Jack's every morning waggling his chartreuse tennis shoes.

***

Now, two days after the grenade incident, I plopped down beside McQuiddy in the swings at Memorial Park. His mom just got him a genuine leather NBA regulation basketball. I watched him petting his new best friend like it was a puppy or something. I swore he was gonna wear the grip off it just by rubbing it all the time. Sweat dripped down his face on account of it being a typical hot, humid Iowa summer day and him practicing for the last two hours at the park basketball court, the one with chain nets on the rims.

"She give you that because she felt guilty about slapping you?" I nodded at his ball.

"No … well … maybe. She felt pretty bad about it."

The Park Commission truck pulled up at the far edge of the little park. The one and only park maintenance man, Duke Doreen, hauled a sandbag and a shovel over to the horseshoe pit to replace the sand gouged out of there by hundreds of matches.

"Geez, Nicky, you're gonna shake the whole swing set down."

McQuiddy referred to my jiggling. If I wasn't jiggling my foot back and forth, I was jiggling my arm, or tapping my foot on the ground or my pencil on the desk. I don't know. I think I just have a lot of extra energy. I can't stand people who sit still for hours at a time, like computer nerds. Geez, I'd go nuts. The swing set was squeaking up a little song to my jiggling.

I spotted the pure hate in McQuiddy's eyes as he watched Duke. "You want me to go kneecap him with my bat?"

"Nah."

"Want to check the memorial?" I asked.

"Nah."

"Talk much?" I worried about the boy when he had no snappy comeback. Not healthy.

In the center of the park, the tallest flagpole between the Mississippi and Missouri rivers displayed a rectangle of the Stars and Stripes as big as the front of my trailer. At night, a spotlight dramatized McGrawsland's one claim to fame. That was the "memorial" part of the park. On the concrete block that held the steel pole, a gray, marble tribute encased in Plexiglas listed all the Iowa boys who had died in the various wars all the way up to Vietnam. Each had a little brass nameplate. They updated it once a month. McQuiddy usually checked it once a week.

A lopsided steel merry-go-round and a slide too hot to sit on in the summer sun rounded out the playground equipment in the area. The one picnic table, over by the horseshoe pit, had long ago shed most of its green paint. The maintenance man, Duke, did the minimum amount of maintenance.

"You told your dad about that Chain Mail Man?"

McQuiddy asked.

"No. Why should I?"

"Good. I just want to talk to him—see what he knows about my dad, okay?"

I grabbed my bat and stuck it in the dirt and gave him the evil eye. "No—it is *not* okay. That man could be dangerous. Did you even notice that weird can smasher he had?"

"Wasn't it cool? How he made it, I mean."

"It looked like a broom handle."

"It was stuck in a coffee can and—filled with concrete." McQuiddy grinned like he'd swallowed a shiner minnow.

"And your point is …?"

"Remember those anchors they made for the boat rentals out at Crystal Lake over by Westridge? Poured concrete into big coffee cans" He didn't wait for my response. "My dad used to work out there as a teen."

"McQuiddy …" I shook my head. When the boy got obsessed like this, it was pretty hopeless. I checked out the new khaki laces he'd put on his canvas tennis shoes. "Can't you just let it be?"

"Let it be? Really? Like you have about the tattoo?"

"Don't *even* say her name, McQuiddy." I slid a hand down my bat and slung it over my shoulder in one threatening move.

"Sorry." He glanced over at me. "You decided where it'll go?"

I brought my bat down. "I thought about the ankle—but I could never go for a swim. How about somewhere on my back, like my shoulder?"

"You're not going to be able to hide it you know, Nicky. In this little town, the news will get to One-Eyed Jack's before the ink's dry."

"So? I don't *even* care, okay?"

"Then put it on your forehead."

"I'm serious, McQuiddy. By the end of this summer I will have her name tattooed on this body, and it'll have the flower right beside it."

My mom's name was Rose.

CHAPTER 5

HENRY

"MOM?"

"NOT ON YOUR life. Davenport's gotten too big," Mom said.

Davenport was hardly what you would call a big city by New York or California standards, but by Iowa standards, nearly a hundred thousand people was a bunch. It was enough of a bunch to include all the good news and bad news of a big city: movie theaters with three screens, nice parks, the levee along the Mississippi, riverboats—and gambling, drugs, crime, and a rough part of downtown, West End.

Nicky's dad invited me to go to Davenport with Nicky and him. Mr. Smithers actually worked out of the American

Civil Liberties Union office there. Folks who needed legal help and had no money went there. Most of them met with Mr. Smithers first so he could figure out which of their lawyers could help them.

"The size of the town's no reason." I used that as a wedge. Mom liked to have good reasons for everything.

"Yes, it is. And besides, there's no adult supervision."

"But—Mr. Smithers?"

"Exactly." She cracked a hint of a smile at her own answer.

"He promised he'd keep an eye on us."

"He lies."

"Oh, right! He lies! What's he lie about, Mom? Does he lie about Nicky's mother being DEAD? Is that what he lies about?" I jumped out of my chair banging my knees against the kitchen table.

"Enough!" She stood up too, almost a foot shorter than me, physically anyway. "I didn't kick your dad out. And I didn't lock the door on him. He left and he—he didn't come back—period."

It took a second for me to catch up. "Why?"

"He had—problems."

"What problems, Mom? What kind of problems did he

have?"

"Bad ones," she said.

"Oh, that really helps!" I noticed she started looking out the window, like she does when she's done talking. I figured I'd get *something* out of this. "So, can I go?"

"Stay away from West End."

Chapter 6

NICKY

MCQUIDDY AND I STOOD in front of the West End Tattoo and Psychic Reading Parlor.

Dad had let us go wander Davenport as soon as we arrived. Dad trusted *me*. It was darn near everybody else he didn't trust.

"Stay away from the levee," he told me. "Lots of our clients hang out there, and not all of them are the good guys."

"This is really crazy, Nicky." McQuiddy's big old eyebrows rose.

Ignoring him, I hesitated at the door of the tattoo shop and *took a breath,* like when I'm batting with bases loaded, and pushed it open. *Dee, dee, dee, dawww!* Some weird notes played in the back of the shop like the music in a mystery movie.

"What's happening?" This teen guy with long, stringy blond hair and arms covered with tattoos looked down at me from his stool behind the counter. I noticed McQuiddy checking out a tattoo of a red and purple dragon coming out from under the guy's shirt and breathing fire on his neck.

"We want to investigate a possible tattoo—for me." I stuffed my hands in my pockets and shifted side to side like I was waiting for the next batter. McQuiddy looked away like he wasn't with this crazy girl.

"Ma!" the kid shouted. "This one's yours."

"Like heck!" came a voice from the back. "I'm eating!"

"Mom!"

"Oh, all right." She pushed aside the beaded strands that hung in the doorway to the back room and her body filled the entrance. She shifted her huge frame with each step and puffed for air. She propped her arms, big as hams, on the countertop and looked down.

"Well, well, well. What do we have here? Kids. Want your palms read?"

"A tattoo," I said.

"Where's your folks?"

"In town."

"Gotta have your folks' permission to get one at your age."

I frowned at McQuiddy.

"Told you." He shrugged his shoulders.

"Actually," I looked up at the lady. "My mom's dead and my dad's in California. Here. Got a permission note from him."

I jammed my hands in my pockets. "Where's that note?" I looked at McQuiddy. "Geez! Left it at home."

McQuiddy closed his mouth tight and puffed up his cheeks. His eyes bulged at me like they were ready to pop out of his head. I knew he had this thing about lies, even though I've caught the boy in a few of his own.

"Sure, little girl." The lady grinned and rolled her eyes at her son. "I believe you."

I pulled two twenty-dollar bills out of my pocket. "I have money."

Both the kid and his mom fixed their eyes on my cash. The mom spoke first.

"Well, if you have permission. What do you think, Amos?"

"It's cool. What do you want?"

"A rose and the name 'Rose.'"

"Cool, Rosie. Where do you want it?"

"Name's not Rosie. It's—it's someone else's name. Besides, I have some questions first. Like where to put it and how hard it is to do."

"You mean," the lady said, "'how much will it hurt,' don't you?"

"No."

"How about …" the lady glanced at McQuiddy as she spoke, "on your neck?" Her grin displayed a few teeth missing.

"No way." McQuiddy spoke up.

"Was I talking to you, beanpole?" the lady said.

"I was thinking it could go on my back," I said.

"Cool," said Amos. "Down around your waist so folks can see it when you wear your bikini."

McQuiddy gave me that puffer-fish-bulging-eyes look again. He wanted to talk so bad but knew I'd knock his block off if he interfered. "Nicky, can I see you outside for a second?" he asked.

"A second," I said.

Outside he blasted me. "Nicky, are you crazy? That is

not a place for kids. It's gross, and the guy's gross, and the lady's gross. Let's go." He pulled my arm.

I didn't budge. I looked back through the shop window.

"Nicky—we'll find another place!" McQuiddy got right in my face.

We heard the music notes as the door opened. Amos frowned at McQuiddy. "It's not *your* business, kid."

"She's my friend."

"It's *her* skin." Amos stepped too close to McQuiddy and me. I could smell his breath, thick with sweet yet putrid smoke.

"Yeah, and her *money*." McQuiddy clenched his jaw and his fists.

Amos clamped his left hand on McQuiddy's shoulder. He had a letter on each knuckle spelling *H-A-T-E*. "Tell you what, kid." Amos squeezed. The boy winced in pain. "You're not invited to the party anymore. Young lady, step inside."

Amos put his right hand on my shoulder. Those knuckles spelled *L-O-V-E*.

I met eyes with McQuiddy. We read each other's mind.

"Ready?" the boy asked.

"Set," I said.

"Go!" McQuiddy hollered.

Simultaneously, we chopped Amos's arms with our fists, breaking free. I spun and hit the sidewalk but came up running. McQuiddy paused a second to give me a lead.

The kid stood in the doorway, like a cow in the rain, moaning in pain.

"Dungbreath!" McQuiddy shot out of there and caught up with me. Only boy in sixth grade could run faster than yours truly.

We ran from West End all the way to the bank clock downtown. I bent over holding my sides and gulped in air. McQuiddy did the same.

"Skinned your knee." He pointed.

"Done worse sliding into home."

"You okay?" he asked.

"My tattoo." I felt this big, empty hole in my gut.

"Look, Nicky," McQuiddy said. "Percy will be down at the levee fishing. He knows stuff, lots of stuff. If anybody can find you a tattoo, he can."

We headed down to the levee to find Percy Gray. Percy was the only black man actually living in McGrawsland. He moved into one of the eight apartment rooms on the edge of town after his wife died a couple years ago. Used to be motel rooms until the Tall Corn Motel closed. Now Percy spent most of his daylight time at the levee in Davenport. It's actually just a twenty-five minute drive from McGrawsland.

When Percy wasn't pulling on one of his fishing lines to feel the nibble of a Mississippi River catfish, he was playing checkers, and when he wasn't playing checkers, he parked himself on one of the benches in front of the rail that held his poles and talked. Actually, he did that all the time, talk. In fact, one time we heard him talking when nobody was around. He was chatting with his wife, Martha, like she was right there. Trouble is, she wasn't there—or anywhere.

Percy's laugh's what I liked. That and his stories. He had this laugh that started real low someplace down in his barrel-size chest, like a growling dog. Then it came up his throat getting louder like a duck call. Finally, it burst into a hacking roar like someone with whooping cough, mouth wide open. That was the best part. His pure gold tooth gleamed in the sunlight.

"Wanna check out Sears?" McQuiddy asked me on the way.

"What?"

"I hear they have a sale on bikinis." He kept a straight

face.

"Shut *up*, McQuiddy!" I took a swing at his shoulder, but he stepped quickly out of range.

"Hey, Percy," McQuiddy whispered.

Percy didn't answer. He was checking one of his bells. He clipped bells on the tips of his rods to play music to him when a catfish decided to taste his big old dew worm or blob of chicken liver. A smelly towel hung off his belt. He used it to wipe his hands after putting on fresh bait or taking off a fish. The chicken liver stains were weeks old. We could smell them from fifty feet away.

As we approached, McQuiddy whispered to me. "Don't bother him right now. He's got a bite."

"You can tell that from here?"

"Toothpick. He sticks one in his mouth whenever he gets a little excited. He douses them in cinnamon paste the day before to give 'em flavor."

I spotted which of the four poles leaning against the rail had the nibble. Percy slowly shuffled over to that one and felt the line. My dad says I could catch a fish in a mud puddle. I don't know about that, but I do know my way around a fishing pole.

"Just a fiddler," Percy let go of the line and addressed

McQuiddy. "Been that way all morning." He nodded at the rope tied to the rail. We looked over the rail. Twelve feet down the old, stone seawall, two small catfish, white bellies up, floated in the river on the loops of the chain stringer at the end of the rope.

Percy rested his arms on the iron rail and gazed out at the river. We joined him. I stared out over the Mississippi at the Rock Island shoreline a mile away. Mom was born over there. An Illinois girl. Dad told me he used to take the old ferry boat across to go on dates with her.

McQuiddy elbowed me.

"What?" I whispered back.

"Your leg," McQuiddy nodded. I had stuck a foot on the second bar of the rail and waggled my knee back and forth. Made the bells on Percy's poles jingle a little. I stopped and gave McQuiddy my *you're-not-my-mother* look.

Percy took a deep breath. "Feel like that old tabby cat of ours." Percy always talked like that—like his wife was still alive. That's the part I didn't like. "Name's Pumpkin Pie, but ain't nothing sweet about him. He sits for hours in front of an old mouse hole, expecting supper cuz three years ago, a little old squeaker poked its head out once too often." The growling started in Percy's stomach. His chest began heaving in and out. "Trouble is, he got so excited, he flipped that little critter straight up in the air and darned if it didn't land in the blouse of my darlin' Martha who was sweeping the floor." The duck call noises started in his throat.

"Whoo-eee! That lady just about tore her clothes off. Ripped her blouse in two pieces and sent that little squealer scrambling right under the door to the back porch."

Percy looked to the heavens. "I tried to take her serious. I really did. First, Martha went after Pumpkin Pie with her broom." Percy exploded, whooping so loud I thought the police might come, or the ambulance. "Then she came after me!" His face turned purple as he gasped for air, his gold tooth gleaming. "Caught me a couple of whacks pretty good. Think for the next little while she changed that cat's name from Pumpkin Pie to Cow Pie."

McQuiddy laughed way too much for that one. He kept his eye on Percy. As Percy pulled out a well-used hanky and wiped a laugh tear from his face, the boy cast his line. "Percy?"

"Henry McQuiddy." Percy remembered everybody's name.

"Seen any signs?"

"Signs?"

"The man on a quest."

"Oh. I see. No, can't say as I have, Henry."

"Anyone pass through here wearing chain mail?" McQuiddy asked.

"Chain mail?"

"You know, like knights wear."

Percy stroked his chin. "Chain mail. No. No, can't say as I have."

"We spotted this vagrant guy who looked like he was wearing something like chain mail over near the Wapsi," I explained as I rolled my eyes at the boy.

"Well, I wouldn't be going around talking to folks like that, I'll tell you that right now." Percy caught McQuiddy looking over at a couple of guys bedded down under some elm trees not far away. Beds were cardboard boxes and raggedy blankets.

"You think *they* might know something?" McQuiddy asked Percy, nodding at the men.

"Don't you be going anywhere near them guys. They tossed all their good sense into the river long time ago."

"Percy?" I spoke up. I had seen him lots, but this was my first time actually talking to him.

"Victoria Smithers," he replied.

"Whhhhhhaaat!" McQuiddy was stunned.

I just about fell over the rail. I thought nobody in the world except Mom and Dad knew. My cheeks burned.

"Is that your real name?" The boy grinned like Percy's cat just swallowing a goldfish.

"Call me *Nicky*," I said to Percy. Changed my nickname from Vicky to Nicky when Mom passed. Only she ever called me Victoria. Besides, that nickname 'Vicky' always reminded me of cough drops, so I made Dad swear to call me only 'Nicky' at Mom's funeral.

"My apologies, Nicky Smithers. How may I help you?"

"You know where I can get a good tattoo?" I ignored McQuiddy's stupid face.

"Well now, young lady, you added a word there that makes that a hard question." He looked at me to see if I got his message.

"Good?" I asked.

"That's the word. Nothing's 'good' about a tattoo. Especially at your age."

"I'm getting one." I looked him right in the eye.

"I see." Again he stroked his chin. "There's a lady out past McGrawsland." Percy turned his huge, brown eyes to

McQuiddy. "Country lady. Name's Dianna. Some say she's a witch doctor. Others say she's just a crazy girl who never got locked up proper. She's okay though. Harmless enough. She does them for special payment."

"Special payment?" I asked.

"Yep. You bring her something special like a picture or some little old trinket and she does you a tattoo."

"What's her address?" I smiled at McQuiddy, who shook his head.

"Don't got one. Lives in an old fixed-up barn three-point-five miles past the new McGrawsland Bridge." Percy eyed us, checking reactions.

I pulled out a ballpoint pen and wrote it down on the palm of my hand.

"Henry McQuiddy, you'll be going with her, won't you?" Percy asked.

"Of course."

Percy nodded.

"If I let him," I added. Boys. They think a girl can't do a thing on her own. Look at McQuiddy's mom. Three stripes on her shoulder—and she kicks butt. What is it with the male animal?

"How, exactly, will we know this place?" I raised my

palm and pen to take notes.

Percy gave me directions. Then, out of the blue, he added, "Say, Nicky Smithers, how's your dad doing these days?"

"Fair to middlin'," I said, but his question hit me hard, like there was some extra weight on it, like he knew something I didn't. Maybe something about how it is to lose your wife.

As we left Percy, I noticed that *I-ate-the-whole-cherry-pie* grin returning to McQuiddy's face. "If you ever say that name to me or to anyone on this planet or any *other* planet, McQuiddy, you're a dead man. Do you hear me?"

"Yes, ma'am." Half his grin remained.

CHAPTER 7

HENRY

"MOM!"

"IT'S TOO FAR, Henry," Mom said. "You're talking about crossing the new McGrawsland Bridge and going clear to Camp Edwards. That's got to be a twelve-mile bike ride."

"Exactly. We want to pack a lunch and make it a quest."

"A *quest*?" she asked.

"Yeah, like Lancelot."

She rolled her eyes. "Just exactly what is the purpose of this quest?"

"Catfish bait."

"What?"

"Percy told us about the place. *I liked to weave a little truth into my lies. Makes them work better.* He has a friend makes his own catfish bait. Supposed to stink so bad the catfish kill each other to get a taste." I kept focused on my hands, flipping a matchbook from the Busy Bea Café between my fingers like a riverboat gambler with a poker chip. I felt her probing eyes on the side of my head, less than three feet away. Close enough to smell her.

Almonds. Mom always shampooed and rinsed with some stuff that smelled like almonds. She ordered it out of a catalogue from New York. She figured it didn't make her smell too girly for her job. But nice.

"What does Nicky's dad say?"

"He said he thought it would be a great adventure." *Never mind that Nicky was using the same line on her dad.*

"Of course." She looked out the window. "Men will be boys."

"Can we?"

"Look, we're getting calls on some homeless man wandering around out by the Wapsi. He seems to be pretty crazy. Big guy. Do *not*—do you copy? Do *not* engage if you see him? And if you have any kind of trouble, go to a farmhouse and call. Okay?"

"Great!"

"Okay?" She put a hand on my shoulder.

"Okay, Mom, sure." I pulled my shoulder away.

***

"Whoa, boy! Where you think you're going?" Nicky said.

I skidded my bike to a stop just in front of the *old* McGrawsland Bridge. "This cuts over a mile off our ride. The new bridge's way out of the way."

The old bridge closed down five years ago, a rickety gathering of old planks and wooden pylons spanning the Wapsi River about a mile past McGrawsland Lake. Folks didn't even use it for walking anymore. The fading *No Trespassing* sign and chain on both sides got the message across to most. In fact, we heard that the last thing to cross it was a runaway pig. The new, concrete and steel bridge was built two miles upstream on the highway bypass.

I watched Nicky wrestle with my words. I knew how bad she wanted that tattoo. Bad as I wanted to find my dad.

"Be there at least a half hour sooner this way," I added.

"Okay, once," she said. "We come back on the new bridge."

"Deal." I lifted the bridge chain for Nicky to wheel her bike under.

The boards under our tires clacked like the dentures of this old guy I know, Joshua Graham Bell, chewing on a day-old donut down at One-Eyed Jack's. He talked about horses, corn, and the meaning of life.

We spotted some guys down below in a flat-bottom wooden boat. Nicky stopped her bike to see how the fishing was. Fishing was about the only thing that could slow that girl down. I pulled up beside her. With wires, metal rods, and a hand crank generator, they *fished.* I had heard of this, knocking out fish with a jolt of electricity, but they usually did it at night when no game wardens were around.

"Hello, Mr. Catfish," said the man cranking the generator. "Time to rise and shine."

Pretty quickly we saw two huge flathead catfish rise to the surface belly up and twitching from the shock. The current didn't take them far because they drifted right into a huge logjam caused by a big cedar that had fallen into the river. The men pulled in their gear and drifted down toward the fish.

One guy looked back over his shoulder. "What're *you* looking at!"

I grabbed Nicky's arm to keep her quiet. Sometimes,

the girl didn't know when to keep her mouth shut. "Let's go, Nicky."

She bent over and snatched a big old rock she found on the bridge.

"Nicky!" I grabbed her wrist and shook the rock free. "Let's go."

"You know that's illegal, what they're doing, fishing with electricity," she said, to *me*, thank heavens.

"I know. But we're not here for that; we're here for a tattoo. Just ignore them."

"They're not talking to me, you know," Nicky said.

"Huh? What?"

"Down there." Nicky pointed to under the bridge.

The men were looking under the bridge. I peered between the boards. His silvery armor shined through. He sat on an old log rocking back and forth like he was rocking a baby. And he was humming.

Nicky spotted him, too. "No, you don't, McQuiddy. This is *my* trip. My tattoo trip. Let's go!"

"Yes, ma'am." I saluted, making a mental note.

***

"Here?" I puffed from the long ride.

"This is where Percy said it would be." Nicky checked

the ink on her palm. "There's the grove of walnut trees."

A well-worn dirt trail led around the trees to an abandoned corn silo. It stood on decaying legs tilting slightly like an old man with a cane. A slight breeze swirled inside the metal cylinder, moaning in complaint. Nicky picked up a fallen walnut and tossed it at the silo. *Clank!* Even the pigeons no longer visited.

Past the silo another hundred feet, an old barn stood at the edge of a cornfield. The door and two windows hinted at it being a residence. A few chickens in the front yard rang the alarm by ruffling up their feathers and running away clucking and scratching to ground like they were announcing intruders.

We stood at the front door.

"You knock," I said.

Knock, knock. Nicky pounded. Nothing.

She knocked again, harder. A fleck of red paint landed on her arm.

The door opened and a young, caramel-colored lady smiled. "Kids! We haven't seen kids in a wad of weeks."

"Hi. You Dianna?" Nicky asked.

"We go by that name. What's yours?" She wore a plain, white muslin men's shirt, which hung down to her knees, and faded blue jeans.

"Nicky."

"And you, Sir Galahad?"

"Name's Henry." I glanced down at her feet. No shoes. *Why'd she call me that?*

She caught me off guard with her next move. She reached out with thin fingers and touched me on the neck. Really.

"Watch it!" I jumped a step backward. Her fingers felt like a crawling spider.

"We is soaked with sweat." She rubbed her fingers together. "And other disturbances."

"Yeah." Nicky nodded at our bikes parked in the chicken yard. "Rode from McGrawsland."

"You here for a treatment?" Her pink lips puckered and twisted a little. Long, straight black hair fell down her shoulders almost to her waist. Her dark brown eyes glistened and gave me the willies.

"Treatment?" Nicky didn't wait for an answer. "No, a tattoo."

"Both of you?"

"Just her." I poked my thumb in Nicky's direction.

"We only gives love tattoos. Got to say that up front."

"Love tattoos?" Nicky asked.

"Tattoos of affection. We don't do ugly, mean things. No skulls."

"It's for my mom."

I couldn't believe she told Dianna that.

"Oh," Dianna said. "Come in."

Nicky charged right in, but I stayed outside.

"McQuiddy!" Nicky shot her warning look that said *You better not desert me now.* I knew that look just as well as her punch. They often came together.

I checked out the place carefully as I stepped onto the wooden floor. Her living room reminded me of this pizza place in Davenport where the tables are all old telephone spools and the floor's covered with sawdust. I looked around for another person or a big dog or a cat because she kept saying "we" and "us," but she seemed to be alone.

"Your mom?" Dianna fixed her eyes on Nicky.

"Yeah."

"You sound sad about it," Dianna said.

"She's dead."

"We see." Dianna gazed into Nicky's eyes. "Oh."

"Oh, what?" Nicky asked.

"We see much—an accident. Bad rain. Your momma

turned to miss the man. Hit the tree."

"Man?" Nicky's face reddened. "It was a deer."

"Oh." Dianna looked away.

Nicky and I glanced at each other with questions on our faces. For several seconds all you could hear was the breathing of three people. The song of a meadowlark out in the fields broke the silence.

"You want the flower with the name?" Dianna asked.

"You know?" Nicky asked.

"A rose, right?"

That's creepy, I thought. *How did she know that? Maybe Percy told her.*

Nicky's arm started shaking. Then I saw something I had never seen on Nicky's face before unless she was really, really mad. Tears.

"It's okay, sweet one. Let those pearls fall. They bless your mommy."

Then Nicky really let out a whoop and cried outright. I just stared at my khaki shoelaces waiting for it to be over with.

"You're a good friend," Dianna said to me.

I felt a lump in my throat. "Yes, ma'am."

She placed a hand on Nicky's shoulder and stroked her

hair with the other hand. "There, there, my sweet one. There, there."

Finally, Nicky quieted herself enough to speak. "Will you do it?"

"It's going to cost you."

Nicky shoved a hand in her pocket, but Dianna caught her wrist. "Not that way."

"How?"

"You have to bring us something."

"Huh?"

I guess Nicky forgot what Percy told us. She was pretty distracted about this tattoo thing, I knew.

"You have to bring us some token of your love for her. Something small but very special to you."

Nicky touched the locket she kept under her blouse. It had her mom's picture in it.

"Not that." Dianna watched Nicky's hand go to her chest. "Nothing as valuable as a locket. Something else." She nodded at a cork bulletin board on the opposite wall. A squad of thumbtacks with mixed-colored plastic heads pinned down a couple of scarves, a pair of pink shoe laces, a little plastic figurine of a black Scotty dog, several postcards, two key chains, a bunch of matchbook covers, a green rabbit's foot, a lock of hair, and the one that really got to me, a set of dog tags off some soldier. I figured they sent them to his girlfriend when he took a VC bullet in the chest. She's probably got a tattoo of his name inside a heart inked on her leg.

Not one coin purse. I squeezed the green, plastic reminder of my dad in my pocket and poked at the note in there with my forefinger.

"You mean, I have to come clear out here again to bring something to you?" Nicky jammed her hands in her pockets and started twisting back and forth.

"Yes. Clear out here." Dianna smiled at her. "Tell you what. We'll do it in water base first, so you can see what it looks like—until your next shower."

"Okay. Um. I was thinking about putting it on my shoulder." Nicky's face added a question mark.

"Let's see." She seemed to be looking around Nicky instead of at her. She put her hands about six inches from Nicky's shoulders and ran them down her sides. "Right—right here." She pointed to Nicky's right foot.

"My foot?"

"It's the one you use to leave Earth," Dianna said.

I attempted to make sense out of what this lady was

saying. *Well,* I thought. *Nicky did leap off that foot to snag high line drives hit down the third baseline. Some kid called her Wrong Foot Nicky—once.*

"Come sit here on our barrel. There. Take off your tennis shoe and sock, please." She pulled down what looked like a fishing tackle box from a shelf and opened it. "This won't hurt at all—but it may tickle."

With a tiny, stiff paintbrush, she dipped into little bottles of paint in the box and dabbed at the top of Nicky's right foot. Her left foot started waggling. Dianna laid the palm of her hand on top of it. "Be still, little foot, your partner will be fine." The lady was talking to Nicky's foot. Really.

I watched Nicky's face. Nicky had these two anger wrinkles that pretty much permanently creased her forehead, even when she smiled. Only her closest friends, like me, knew she wasn't really mad. Well, those wrinkles smoothed out as Dianna worked. Nicky looked—well, nice—peaceful. Her whole body seemed to settle down like a cat curling up and going to sleep on a sunny porch.

I felt it, too. Peaceful. Like when my fishing bobber's sitting still on a glass-smooth lake turned gold by sunset.

"Okay," Dianna lifted Nicky's foot, bending her knee so

she could see it up close.

A huge grin crossed Nicky's face. "That's it. Look, McQuiddy."

A tiny red rose on a thorny branch with a few leaves seemed to grow out from between her big toe and the next one. Above that, old-style lettering published her mom's name in red, outlined in blue.

Rose

"Just let it dry a bit and you can put your sock on," Dianna said. "It's latex base, so it can last a good while. Plenty of time to decide about a permanent one."

When we left, Nicky and Dianna hugged for a long time. I, on the other hand, couldn't wait to get out of there. I didn't want her to start talking her voodoo talk about Dad. My dad was alive, and nobody was going to tell me different.

CHAPTER 8

NICKY

FOR ME, FRIDAY NIGHT meant my first chance to show off my tattoo to the only other human being in McGrawsland who knew about it. For everyone else, Friday meant one thing, *fresh pie day* at the Busy Bea. Busy Bea Café's our one and only restaurant. It sits at the end of Main Street and serves homemade pie so good that the truckers drive six miles off the freeway on an old two-lane, potholed obstacle course to get a slice. The empty field at the end of Main makes perfect truck stop parking. Just for Friday's, Bea hired Terrence Ashton to help wait tables. They squeezed in four extra card tables and metal folding chairs for all the truckers tromping in for a taste of heaven. Terrence had a way with the guys. He always knew just what to say to put a smile on their faces. "Nice rig. You could shave your face using those rims as mirrors." That kind of thing.

Although pie day started at ten in the morning, most of the locals showed up there sometime after supper for dessert. It was lemon meringue and chocolate cream pie night and Queen Bea, as she was called, made them with real lemons and dark chocolate from Switzerland. She packed the crust with fresh butter. Dad and I had just taken our first bite, which was dissolving in our mouths like ambrosia, when McQuiddy and his mom jangled the cowbells on the door.

Everyone in town knew about the unspoken war between our parents. I noticed Queen Bea rolled her eyes as they entered. Her way of saying she had two bulls in her china shop.

Dad pulled the newspaper to his face when he spotted McQuiddy's mom passing by. His two big hands gripped the edges of the paper firmly, like he was driving a tractor on a bumpy field. I halfway expected smoke to come out his ears. All I could see were the blond curls on top of his head. Got my red hair from Mom.

As they passed by, McQuiddy and I just nodded at each

other.

Doris McQuiddy wore one of her typical going-to-town dresses, a pale blue one with tiny purple flowers. The pretty cobalt-blue scarf she wrapped around her neck made her look real classy and showed off her long, straight blond hair. She turned some truckers' heads. But none of them dared to comment. A newbie did once and got an earful from Sheriff's Sgt. Doris McQuiddy.

McQuiddy kept trying to get her to wear jeans like everybody else. I think he was just embarrassed at how pretty his mom was. Personally, I liked how she looked even though I'm not a dress kind of girl. I've been looking at some pictures in ladies magazines lately and wondering how that stuff would look on me. Wished I could still hang out with Mrs. McQuiddy like I used to. I still had no idea what happened between her and my dad.

She led McQuiddy to a booth at the other end of the place pretending she didn't notice Dad and me. That meant they were exactly three booths away. Busy Bea was a small hive.

As soon as they got their slices of pie, I heard McQuiddy ask his mom if he could sit outside. We had this unspoken agreement with our parents so we could get together on pie night. I waited about sixty seconds and asked my dad the same question.

McQuiddy looked up as I jangled the cowbells going out the door. He sat on one side of the wooden bench in front of the store window with his pie in his lap. A solitary light bulb beamed about ten feet above him as a beacon to the sweet tooth. It was the only thing close to a streetlight in McGrawsland. It used to be a yellow bug-bulb, but most of the paint had worn off and the lacey wings of mayflies danced around it, twirling like little girls at a birthday party. Crickets chirped incessantly on the walls below. A chilly, breeze warning of rain interrupted the warm summer night.

"Look." I nodded at my foot as I scooted beside the boy on the bench. I wore sandals with wide leather straps on the top. I unbuckled my right sandal and there it was, still bright and clear, "Rose," with a beautiful little rose below it.

"Cool," McQuiddy said.

"I'm keeping this one as long as I can."

"Dianna said *a while*."

"I know." I gave him my mad dog look. "Kept it outside the shower curtain last night."

"Thought I smelled something." McQuiddy grinned

and braced his shoulder.

I punched it, but not that hard.

"Ow!" He rubbed it, faking pain. "Soon as you get it wet, it's gone."

"Thank you so much for your words of wisdom, McQuiddy." I showed him the rubber glove with the fingers cut off that I'd wear on my foot when it rained. "And shut up."

"Yes, ma'am."

Over his shoulder I spotted two big boots, caked with dried mud, tromping out of the shadows across the street. My head tilted up as the man shuffled forward, and his pale, blue eyes and metallic vest gleamed in the light.

"McQuiddy!" I grabbed my boy's arm.

"What?" McQuiddy glanced down at my hand.

"That!" I pointed.

The man's shuffle turned into a march as he crossed the street headed on a collision course for us. His old, black army boots, caked with mud, stomped on the concrete. Under his camouflage U.S. Army field jacket, he wore a long-sleeved flannel shirt, dirt-brown. Probably hadn't changed it in years. His blue jeans had turned black. Except for his eyes and a forehead creased with worry, his face hid in a mush of scraggly, dark brown hair.

But that was nothing. Covering his shirt, all the way down to his belt, was that chain mail vest. For the first time, in the light of the bulb, I saw exactly what it was made of—hundreds of circles of metal pop-tops, the kind that usually stay attached to pop cans.

The man came to a halt, *one-two*, right in front of McQuiddy. He pulled something out of a front pocket of his field jacket and dropped it on the sidewalk between our boy's feet. Good thing no bugs came down to our level, because McQuiddy would have swallowed them all. His mouth gaped open like a baby crow's.

The guy pointed the toe of one boot on the ground behind him and did an about-face. He never looked down the whole time. *Hup-two-three-four*, he marched away. His eyes looked straight ahead as if nobody else existed in the entire world. *For this man*, I thought, *that's true.* Then I saw something—for a split second, just as McQuiddy was picking up the object between his feet—the man turned just his head and looked back at the boy.

I grabbed McQuiddy's denim shirt and whispered, "What's that?"

The boy lifted the object to his lap. A red ribbon with a

blue stripe down the center wrapped around a bronze star at the bottom.

"It's my dad's. He got this from my dad."

"McQuiddy, he looked right at you," I said. "You think he *is* your dad?

"Nah, he looks nothing like him."

"Sir? Excuse me." McQuiddy tried to stand, but I yanked him down by his shirttail.

"Sir?" McQuiddy tried again. The man continued his focused, shuffling march.

"I never thought I'd be saying this, Henry McQuiddy, but you were right," I whispered. "That *is* chain mail. You see what it's made of?"

The boy frowned. "Can I have my shirt back, please?"

"Stay down, boy." I tried to distract him. "Whew! He smelled gross."

"Swamp muck," he said. "And BO."

"Makes me gag."

McQuiddy lunged to his feet knocking away my hand. "Watch out!"

Screeeeeeeeeeeeeeeeeeeech! Tires screamed at the Chain Mail Man. A green Chevy pickup fishtailed to a stop one foot from his knees. He continued crossing the street, eyes straight ahead.

"Geez Louise!" I said. Dust and tire smoke filled the air.

Duke Doreen stuck his head out the truck window. "Get the hell out of the road, ya' Big Loony!"

"Leave him alone!" McQuiddy started toward the curb.

"Oh, no, you don't." I jumped to my feet, ready to tackle the boy.

Clankity, clankity, clank! The cowbells rattled ferociously as the café door opened. McQuiddy's mom came storming out. "You kids all right?"

Behind her came my dad. "Nicky, get over here!"

Mrs. McQuiddy peered out into the darkness of the street. The light bulb above the café illuminated the chain mail on the man. He was across the street headed away.

"You all right?" Mrs. McQuiddy hollered at the man.

He paused, turned his head slightly in her direction, but he didn't look. He took a big breath, let it go, and headed for the cornfields.

"You know him, Mom?" McQuiddy pointed.

"Not really." She aimed her green laser eyes at her son and fired. "Let's go." She shot a hot beam at Dad and pulled the boy's arm.

"Bye." I held up a hand, palm out, like an Indian

farewell. My dad's huge hand locked on my shoulder, trembling a little. It said *You're not going anywhere but with me.* He worried about losing the second love of his life. Yours truly.

As I glanced away, I could barely make out the shiny chain mail headed for the cornfields. A few sprinkles of rain touched my face, and some distant thunder rumbled warning of a heavier downpour. The smell of burning tire rubber lingered in the air and my nose. I could even taste it—a sickening taste. I couldn't help but think about my mom's crash.

Told Dad I needed to use the restroom before we left. In there, I took out my rubber glove and pulled it onto my right foot. I reread her name and admired the beautiful rose. I stretched the white rubber protection on top of it. I was ready for the Iowa rain.

CHAPTER 9

HENRY

BY THE TIME MOM and I got to the front porch of our trailer, tiny raindrops sounding like thousands of BBs pelted the tin roof. I spotted something sitting on the top step. Quivering in the blowing rain, three wild daisies crowded through the small hole of a pop can.

"What's *that*?" Mom asked.

"I—I don't know. A gift, maybe?" I searched Mom's eyes.

"Well, it sure as shootin' isn't for me," she said. "Toss it."

I just knew the Chain Mail Man had left his calling card. I waited until my mom headed for her room, brought the can of flowers in, filled it with fresh water, and put it on the kitchen table. That's when I noticed the pop-top missing.

I wasn't about to tell Mom about the Bronze Star. I hid it in my tackle box. She had enough to handle with her job, the big cow of a sheriff, and a son she couldn't corral. Besides, I was sure I was close and wanted to show her that I could find him.

***

I woke up staring at the noisy ceiling, my head throbbing from a migraine. Flashes of light around my eyes put me in a whole different world of pain. Marbles of rain pounded the roof—drenching rain, rain that soaked everything and everybody exposed to it. I propped up on one elbow and looked out my window. Clouds crowded the sky like black-robed witches huddled over their bottomless cauldron, spilling buckets of rain. It was a witch who told Lancelot he had a kid, Sir Galahad. I'd been reading about that stuff since Dianna called me that name. Weird lady.

Anyway, there were no silver linings, no rainbows, no breaks in the rain until the witch's spell broke. But worst of all, in McGrawsland, rain meant no place for a kid to go. Well, there's your best friend's house; that is, if your best friend's dad and your mom weren't mortal enemies. The black knight and the white knight. Haven't quite figured out which is which.

In the summer, I always managed to get up before Mom—because of the prospect of schools of fish rather than a school of kids. This morning, however, it was thoughts about chain mail that woke me. That and a throbbing head. The rain continued to pound our metal roof like a thousand steeds galloping into battle. I got to the kitchen a good half hour before Mom, took my migraine meds, and got her coffee perking, knowing she had a Saturday shift. I'd make her pancakes on Sunday.

The soda can and flowers had been disposed of, probably during one of my mom's midnight forays to the fridge. I figured she'd do that. But I had a Plan C. *C* was for cans, six pop cans in the trash. Trash went out Monday. I dug them out, shook off potato peels, and wiped off the coffee grounds with a paper towel.

I thought about this all night. *How did the Chain Mail Man make his chain mail?* I got a pair of needle-nose pliers from my tackle box and snipped a cut into the side of one of the pop-top loops. I took another loop and pushed the edge through the slit linking the two loops together. I linked all six loops into a little aluminum bracelet and carefully set it on the kitchen table—at Mom's place.

I poured myself a bowl of frosted cereal and waited, pretending to read all the fascinating material on the back of the box. I glanced up at her, then purposely did not look again as she approached the table.

"Hi, Mom."

She was already decked out in full uniform with eight different weapons and devices on her belt. Her black boots clacked on the kitchen floor. Her eyes darted around the kitchen. "Have you seen my blue scarf anywhere? Don't remember where I …"

I knew she'd spotted my little gift. I felt it. That special electricity filled the room, like the Iowa air right after the flash of lightning and right before the thunderclap.

She'd pulled out her baton. I cringed expecting her to hit something with it. Maybe me. Instead, she pointed the baton at the chain mail, and, with the tip, shoved it off the table and into the wastebasket.

"What the hell do you think you're doing?" she said.

"I just …" I jumped up to retrieve the links and banged my knees into the table knocking half the cereal out of my bowl.

"You just stay the hell out of my private life!"

"*Your* private life!" I swiped at some syrupy milk on my

shirt with a kitchen towel. "What about my life?"

"You spoiled little brat! Who do you think put that box of cereal on the table?" She pointed with her baton.

"Here." I shoved the box of cereal toward her. "You can have it back."

"I am really not up for this bull!" She latched her baton to her belt and stood up to leave.

"You know him, don't you? He's a friend of Dad's."

The kitchen door slammed her answer. She left her coffee.

My hands shook, and I tried three times before I finally swallowed the gob of cereal I still held in the side of my mouth through all that.

Mom knows him. I was sure. Her face couldn't lie. Her angry tears. I couldn't remember the last time I saw her cry. I felt physically sick to my stomach about that, about Mom, I mean—but I had to know. Dad said he'd return, *no matter what.* I looked at his picture on the wall. *No, that guy looked nothing like him.*

I stared out the kitchen window. The rain had paused, and a sliver of sunlight squeezed through the clouds. Raindrops adorned the glass pane like jewels on a king's robes. *Did the Chain Mail Man really know my dad? Why did he wear that vest? Was he on a quest too? And where did he go when it rained like this?* Then it dawned on me. *I knew!*

I picked up the phone. "Nicky, get your raincoat on. There's something we've got to check out."

"Right," she said. "Your mental condition."

"Just meet me at Fast Mart—bye." I hung up before she could argue.

This time, I didn't call Mom to let her know where I was going. I figured I'd already caused her enough grief for one day. We'd be home before she got back from work. I forgot all about my migraine.

Chapter 10

NICKY

I SIPPED THE HOT-chocolate bribe McQuiddy handed me and sat on the bench in the back of Fast Mart by the bathrooms. He took a big swallow. A nice mustache of chocolate foam spread across his upper lip from corner to corner of his mouth. Made the boy look more mature than he really was, which wasn't hard to do.

"So here's the deal—and don't go ballistic on me, Nicky. Mom already did that. I thought this out." Two long swipes of his tongue, back and forth, wiped his upper lip clean like a windshield wiper. His eyebrows rose.

"Oh, great! So let me guess. You're here right now without your mom's permission."

McQuiddy's jaws bulged. "Look, I've already ticked her

off once today …"

"So?"

The boy struggled. "Okay, look. She lied to me, see. About my dad, I mean."

"Oh, I see. And you've never lied to *her*, Mr. Catfish Bait?" I reminded.

"Did you want me to tell her about your tattoo then?"

I ignored his question. "If this is about that guy, McQuiddy, you can forget it."

"I know where he is—right now."

"Goody for you."

"Nicky, we gotta check it out."

I shook my head looking down at my red rubber boots. "We gotta call the Wizard, McQuiddy, to get you a brain."

"I got this feeling, Nicky. He knows my dad. That medal was my dad's." He knew the dad thing beat all other plays. Mine, of course, was the mom thing.

"Geez, McQuiddy! Do you remember that pounding thing he had? Do you care at all that this guy is obviously extremely unstable?"

"I think he left us flowers—on our porch," he said.

"Flowers?"

"Yeah. In a soda can."

"You had flowers on your porch in a soda can?" I had to check reality with this boy.

"From the guy—the Chain Mail Man."

"That guy doesn't even know how to walk across the street."

"The can. Pop-top was missing." He looked me in the eye.

"Okay, okay. But—why would he do that?" I asked.

"Like I said, I think he knows my dad. My theory is they were army buddies."

"Geez." I shook my head. "Where're we going?" At this point, I could no longer hold back a thought that had been niggling in my brain for days now. *What if this guy is McQuiddy's dad, and the boy just doesn't recognize him.* Gotta admit, though, he didn't look anything like the Mr. McQuiddy I remembered.

"Under the old McGrawsland Bridge. It's the only dry place around here when it rains, except for the shelter of the gas pumps at Fast Mart."

"Tell me you're kidding, McQuiddy. Please. Cuz if you don't, I must certify you as totally insane. Not a marble left in your head."

"Very funny," he said.

"No," I said. "It is *not* funny in any way. Do the words "No Trespassing" mean anything to you?"

"He's there, Nicky. I feel it in my bones. I gotta know."

A loud crack from nearby lightning unzipped the clouds, and a torrent of rain pelted everything like bullets. McQuiddy tossed his paper cup, pulled on his plastic hood, and stepped out into it.

"Right." I checked out the boy as I pulled on my hood. I saw something on his face that tugged at me like a kindergarten kid pulling on your pant leg wanting the bathroom. His pain was urgent. The boy missed his dad, much as I missed Mom. I mean, who knows what I'd be up to if I thought my mom was alive somewhere? I knelt down and tightened the buckles on my boots. "We get my tattoo wet and you die."

As we sloshed through the muddy street riddled with rain and headed for the old bridge, all I could see was the back of his camouflage raincoat. *Why, oh why, do I follow this boy?*

Chapter 11

HENRY

NICKY AND I STOOD at the condemned bridge for a moment, scanning the area. Raindrops drummed on my camouflage, plastic poncho like a charging battalion of shouting foot soldiers. The rush of the rising river swept tree branches, planks, plastic bottles, and other debris downstream like the casualties of that charge. The water turned that gray-brown mud color you get when you mix every can of leftover paint together, the same color I had painted the steps to our trailer.

We stepped past the *No Tres__sing* sign. Some of the black, block letters had surrendered to Iowa weather.

Nicky frowned at me as we stepped over the chain blocking the entrance to the bridge. She grabbed the bridge rail and leaned over, searching for our guy.

"No, not here," I shouted. "The other side. There's a big flat area under the bridge over there. That's where we saw him the other day."

"This is stupid," Nicky said. "Suicidal."

"Just follow me, okay?"

"You expect us to cross that!?" She pointed at the boards coated with a thin, slick sheen of running water caused by a torrent of exploding rain bombs.

"Hold tight. Step sideways." I led the way grabbing the rail and side-stepping across.

Nicky followed, keeping her legs under her with the support of her home-run-hitting arms. The bridge groaned and trembled with the rush of water assailing its wooden pylons. Sheets of rain blotted our view.

A little more than halfway across, my leg plunged through the floor of the rotting bridge all the way up to my thigh. Nicky's arms caught me under my armpits. She nearly went down with me. Half a broken plank plunged into the river. My knee and thigh burned from the scrape as I pulled it out.

"That's it, McQuiddy! We're going back."

"*We* are not going anywhere." I turned my pain into a

hateful glare. "You go back."

"What?" she shouted.

"I said *you* go back."

She looked at me like she was trying to figure out if I was for real. "Right." She turned away. "I'm outta here."

I'd never seen a look like that on her face. My words had cut her heart.

My throat tightened like when I read that note from my dad. Like there was a hangman fitting my neck for a noose. I was waiting for the thumbs-down from the queen. My throat throbbed. I swallowed hard. "Nicky, wait!"

She stopped, keeping her back to me. Then she continued. One foot slipped out from under her. She pulled herself back up with her hands gripping the rail.

"Nicky, please!"

"What!?" She glared back at me.

"I smell something." I pointed to the floor of the bridge. "Smoke. From down there." I think I did. Or did I make it up? I was so desperate.

"I can't smell anything."

"Over here! It's a campfire."

"Geez Louise." Nicky made her way back to me shaking her head. Felt like I got the queen's thumbs-up, *Let him live.* My throat relaxed.

I put a hand on her shoulder. "Smell it?"

"No." She frowned at my hand on her shoulder, which I instantly took away. "So now what?"

"So we talk to him." I gripped the rail and leaned over it. "Hey, Dad!"

"What? Did you just call him *Dad*, McQuiddy?"

"No."

"You did, too."

"No way."

"You know he can't hear us in this rain, right?"

At the end of the bridge, a steep trail of mud led under the bridge, a fisherman's trail, for sure. In this rain, it became a waterslide.

Nicky pointed at the slick path. "Now can we go back?" The huge drops continued to pound our plastic hoods.

"I can grab those bushes." I could barely make them out in the sheets of rain.

"Really?" Nicky stabbed me with her look. "Bushes?"

"I'll be back." I sat on my rear end and pushed with my hands.

I slid about ten feet before I shot out my hand. I caught a good branch of a strong berry bush. *Berry bush!* That explained my pain. The thorns dug into my hand. But I held on. The other option was worse. The river churned.

"Hey, Nicky!" I hollered up to her. "Stay there! I'll be right back."

"No way, McQuiddy!"

"Just let me check. I'll signal if he's there."

"Ten seconds."

"What?"

"You've got ten seconds to find out."

"Okay. Right."

I eased myself to the edge of the river clutching the root of another shrub. The bank cut straight down from there.

On hands and knees, I peered under the bridge. In the blackness I spotted the glow of a small campfire. It highlighted bushy hair covering the man's head and face—and glistened off his chain mail. He hunched up in a ball in front of the fire rocking back and forth.

"Hey!" I waved my free hand.

The Chain Mail Man turned, jaws clenched, vest shining in the firelight.

"Do you know Lance?"

I couldn't hear him, but in the firelight I saw his mouth

move. It formed the word, "Lance."

"Eeeeeyikes!" Nicky came sliding down and bashed into me. We plunged into the river.

I hit the water kicking my feet and flailing my arms, trying to pull my head above the raging water. A whirlpool pulled me away from shore and sucked me under and dragged me downstream. I pulled myself back to the surface and scanned the river. I spotted Nicky behind me. She gasped for air and flailed her arms like a wounded duck. She dipped under. Even Nicky couldn't fight these currents.

The river spun me in powerful eddies created by strong currents curling around big snags of rock and fallen trees. I spotted her again now in front of me.

"Nicky …" I swallowed a big gulp of sour water. A whirl of current pulled me under, twisted and turned me, and filled my nose with bubbling mud soup. I opened my eyes. Dark, brown water cut off my vision. I tried to swim to the surface and ended up sticking a hand in the muddy bottom. I pushed off.

I broke the surface and caught a gulp of air. The river seemed to get mad at me, pulling me down and spinning me like a little toy top. My lungs begged for more air. My body tumbled.

Holy cow! Something grabbed me. The tangle of an underwater snag latched onto me. I fought to get free with visions of a giant squid. I doubled over and groped to untangle a mass of tentacle-like roots clutching my feet. Out of breath, I gave one last thrust upward.

I burst to the surface right in front of a logjam. I flung my arm and caught a branch with a bloody hand, swallowing big gulps of air. I gagged between gasps from the putrid taste of the river. I pulled my head above the logjam and stretched my neck. No sight of Nicky.

I scrambled on top of a thick tree branch. It caught planks, reeds, chunks of Styrofoam, and one dead carp quivering on the surface in the current as though it were still alive.

On the other side, the river raged on. I scanned every log, every piece of debris in the river hoping Nicky had found a life-saving float. Nothing.

A big head popped to the surface. His arms thrashed. His chain mail vest mirrored rare glimpses of sunlight from the breaking clouds.

His legs churned up brown froth like a paddle wheel.

Nicky's head bobbed up ten yards in front of him. She

stabbed at the air and disappeared. I had this sickening thought—*it was like she was waving goodbye.*

"Nicky! Nicky!" The noise of the river swallowed my words.

The Chain Mail Man dived after Nicky.

Sucking in my breath and holding it, I counted … *one, two* … *seventeen, eighteen, nineteen* … Nicky and I once had a breath-holding contest at the municipal swimming pool in Davenport. It was a tie.

Forty-seven, forty-eight, forty-nine … . I felt that pin-prickling tingling in my head. *Hundred thirty-five, hundred thirty-six* … *Ppppuuuhhhh!* I let go and drew a breath. That was our record.

Come up, Nicky! Please, come up! I scoured the surface.

A good fifty yards past where they went under, two heads bobbed to the surface. The Chain Mail Man wrapped one arm around Nicky's waist and stroked the water with the other.

Before them, just the top branches of an underwater cottonwood tree that had fallen into the river waggled a few feet above the surface. Currents spun the pair away from the tree branches, but the Chain Mail Man kicked up a splash that propelled them back toward the tree. Nicky grabbed it. The man missed. His head drifted on down the river like a cork fishing bobber, getting smaller and smaller and finally getting sucked around the bend, out of sight.

"Hold on, Nicky!" I shouted. She couldn't hear me. I straddled the tree trunk and waved both hands. "Nicky! Over here!" Couldn't see me either. She clung to her treetop like an ant to a floating leaf.

I gave up calling and scrambled toward shore through the slippery branches of the tree. My shoulder ached and my hand burned. The trunk I clung to quivered in the power of the current.

"No way!" The *wounded soldier* part of me said that, the part that thinks life's not fair. Well, my life anyway. The trunk I was on disappeared underwater a good twenty feet from shore. Roiling water double-dared me. Jumping in here would be like spitting my gum into a flushing toilet.

I surveyed the situation. Lots of smaller branches grew out of the trunk I was on. I looked down. The river bubbled with sarcastic laughter. *You'll never make it,* it seemed to say.

I saw what I needed to do. I wrapped my legs around the trunk of the tree and eased into the raging water. I stuck my arms under, feeling for a branch. Got one.

What I planned to do was let go of the trunk and use the branches underwater to swing myself to shore, like Tarzan swinging on the vines. Trouble was, my legs wouldn't let go. They trembled and squeezed harder.

My heart ached, I mean, it physically hurt, like somebody grabbed my chest and squeezed hard. "Blast it, legs. Let go!"

I felt beaten. Beaten by my own legs. I had these weird thoughts: *If he really loved Mom, why didn't Dad find a way to get back to us? Was it me? I'm a liar and a quitter. Heck, I won't even try out for the basketball team, and I know I'm good. Who'd want a kid like that? I just give up—like my dad did.*

"*That* guy didn't give up." I said out loud.

But now, as I looked down the river, the Chain Mail Man had disappeared around the bend. He saved Nicky's life. Well, almost anyway. She was hanging onto a tree in the middle of the river. My chest burned more with just one thought: She's my friend! "Ready or not, legs, we're doing this." I lunged toward the underwater branch with two hands and grabbed it.

It swung me toward shore with the river pummeling my face so hard I couldn't breathe. I wasn't close enough. I let go with one hand to search for another underwater branch.

I nabbed a small one. When I grabbed the little branch with the other hand, the weight of my body snapped it off, and I was shot down the river just a few feet from shore.

My arms and legs flailed like windmills and I thought I was a goner. My hand latched onto a tree root growing out of the shoreline. I grabbed it with both hands and pulled myself to shore. I managed to climb the slippery mangle of roots after several tries and dragged myself through the mud to a grassy knoll.

Hang on, Nicky.

I stood and ran—three strides. *Wham!* My back and head smacked the ground hard. My feet had slipped out from under me on wet grass. I fought a dizzy feeling and gasped for air. I lay in mud and slippery grass, rain pelting my face. I'd have to crawl.

I flipped over like a turtle, dug my elbows into the earth, and pulled. I pushed with my knees. I crawled, not like a baby, but like a soldier does under barbed wire. Somewhere in the back of my brain crept a vague memory that my dad had taught me to crawl like this. My body remembered it. I was just five—right before Dad left for Vietnam.

Not far down the shoreline, I spotted her. I pulled

myself up by the elbow of a small tree branch. "Nicky!" I waved. "Over here!"

She started to wave back. The current yanked her body away from the branches. She grabbed for a stem with her left hand, her glove hand, and caught it. Not much got by that hand. *Thank God,* I thought.

Nicky pulled herself back to the branches and wrapped her legs around one. "I can't make it!" She wasn't that far from shore—but far enough.

"Just hold on!" I yelled. "I'll be right back!"

A huge cottonwood had toppled from the shore and disappeared into the river pointed toward Nicky. Those branches Nicky clung to were part of this tree. Its roots clutched at the bank like a bunch of fat, angry snakes. Brown froth between us reminded me of my hot-chocolate bribe to get her to come with me. My stomach churned with guilt.

I felt the ground tremble. The huge root mass seemed to groan, like it was preparing to launch the entire tree, and Nicky, down river.

"Hold on, Nicky!" I scrambled into the woods searching. It was like scanning a crowd for a familiar friend. Among the drab cedar and oak, I spotted my target. It seemed to gleam with its own light. A fallen birch sapling stretched fifteen feet on the ground like a defeated knight's jousting pole. I dragged it back.

Wrapping my legs around the cottonwood trunk, I shimmied down to where it entered the water, dragging the birch sapling behind me, and grabbed a small branch for support. I felt the trunk vibrating in the raging torrent. I extended the birch rod. "Nicky! Grab the end of this and hold on."

"What!?"

"Grab the pole!"

While straddling the trunk like a bull rider, I fed the small end of the pole out into the water. I struggled to keep it vertical when it dipped into the current. I could barely see Nicky hidden in the quaking leaves out there. Then I felt it. Like a fish bite. My pole quivered.

"You got it?!"

"Yes!"

I tried to let the pole swing slowly. I really did. The current was too strong, and Nicky arched toward shore in seconds and smashed against the muddy bank.

"Ow! My head!"

"You okay?" I shouted.

"Oh, just peachy!" She spit out some mud, dark as her Black Jack gum.

"Grab the roots on the bank!" I shimmied backward back up the trunk of the cottonwood.

"I got 'em!" she hollered.

I reached shore, released the birch pole, crawled over to Nicky, and extended a hand.

"Gotcha!" I pulled her up.

We both fell on our backs, exhausted, unable to move, looking up at a thick umbrella of cottonwood leaves. The rain quit, just like that. Dripping leaves added punctuation. My shoulder ached. My hand burned. I turned my head and saw a knot on the side of Nicky's head.

We didn't speak for a while. We both gulped for air like carp at the surface of a stagnant pond sucking in life.

"You okay?" I asked.

"Yeah—I think so. You?"

I held up my bloody hand and examined it. "Stable."

"Right." She turned her head and glanced at my face. "Your face is as black as a jungle soldier," she said.

"Yours too."

The ground trembled and we heard a sound like a big groan. It was the big cottonwood in the middle of the river that had held Nicky. The current ripped it up by the roots and carried it down river.

I wrapped my arms around my chest thinking about what I would have done if Nicky had still been on that tree. She never would have made it. Like my dad.

Then Nicky said, "You crying, McQuiddy?"

"Heck, no."

"He might have made it. Powerful swimmer," Nicky said.

"Yeah, maybe."

"Check it out." She nodded at her feet.

Her rubber boots had been ripped from her feet. The tattoo was gone.

"Sorry."

"Me too." Nicky took a deep breath. "We'd better go."

"Yeah." I glanced at where the raging river disappeared around the bend, the spot where I last saw the man in the chain mail vest. I wondered if I'd ever see him again.

But what I wondered even more than that was something else. Something that just sort of snuck up on me. I wondered if Nicky would still be my best friend when we got to junior high school. Assuming we made it to junior high school. I wondered if I would lose Nicky, like I lost my dad.

I felt a hard punch on my shoulder. "You *are* crying."

She thought I was crying about him. She was only half right.

CHAPTER 12

NICKY

NEXT MORNING, I CALLED the boy while we watched WOC-TV's local news, which stood for "Wonders Of Chiropractic" because the station came out of Palmer College of Chiropractic in Davenport. I always thought it was cheating that they used the "O" in "of" as part of the station letters. "*Ofs*" shouldn't count—too small. Anyway, there was no news of storm victims.

"He could still be alive," McQuiddy said.

"Yeah," I said. "Sure."

The rain had let up, but it was way too soon to go very far looking for anybody. It'd be at least another day before the roads cleared and banks of the river dried up enough to walk the edge. Even Percy and the old guys who went to

Davenport to fish the Mississippi stayed home. So McQuiddy and I met at the other big hotspot of McGrawsland, One-Eyed Jack's, the center for town gossip.

"Hey, Nicky." When old Jack winked, he couldn't see at all, because his bad eye was covered by a black patch.

Years ago, just before he opened the new store, Jack decided he'd try that fancy Montana fly fishing instead of regular old Iowa bait fishing. He got himself a fly rod and tried flipping a popper fly way out between the trees in the center of the lake, hoping to bring some big bluegill up to the top. Well, the fourth time he swung back that skinny little willow rod, his fly hooked an unexpected target—his own eye—thus the name of Jack's store.

Folks made up reasons to go the hardware store, like needing a new plastic cover for a wall socket. They were really after any morsel of local news they could chew on at the supper table. Except for early morning when Terrence sat there alone, there were always three and sometimes as many as eight guys hanging around on the benches in front of the store, sipping free coffee that Jack brewed every morning and eating day-old donuts picked up at the Busy Bea one block down the street. The guys said the coffee matched the price.

Jack never let on, but he paid Terrence to open up the place and turn on the coffee Jack had set up the night before. Terrence told me. That's why, by nine o'clock, the coffee was already a bit thick. It was three hours old.

Today, however, the soggy conditions drove everyone indoors. McQuiddy and I pretended to be looking at toilet fixtures, a good spot to put an eye and ear on the conversation. I caught the boy checking out Duke Doreen. He hated Duke more than poison ivy, which the boy got once wiping his butt with the leaves down by the old swimming hole.

It wasn't his hearing aids tucked under a mop of long, orange hair that caused him to yell. Duke just shouted when he talked, like nobody would pay attention to him otherwise.

"Got one big rig down in the ditch by my place. They had to call in a giant tractor from the John Deere plant in Bettendorf to wench it out of there." Duke took a puff on his homemade Prince Albert cigarette. "Stupid trucker." His shoulder muscles rippled beneath the white knit long-johns top he wore under his bib overalls. He sipped from a Styrofoam cup of black coffee and shuddered at the taste.

"Nothing could maintain equilibrium on that road

when precipitation's that heavy," proposed Joshua Graham Bell, the oldest of the bunch. They called him "The Professor," on account of his years in college and his vocabulary. "One can't differentiate between a pothole and a puddle." His head was a frizz of white hair with matching beard and mustache.

"Someone said they thought they saw Big Loony taking a dip in the Wapsi in the worst part of the storm. You hear anything about that Professor?" one of the other men asked.

I elbowed McQuiddy. To my shock, he jabbed a return message.

I rubbed my arm.

"Indeed," Joshua replied. "Celia Caldwell reported his swift passage past her residence. My theory is he took refuge under the old bridge and perhaps fell asleep. Wapsi rises more rapidly than an obstructed toilet in a storm like that." Joshua glanced over at the toilet aisle and spotted McQuiddy and me. "But now that we've exhausted that topic, let's move on to cabbages and kings."

"Should of been locked back up." Duke spit a loose strand of his cigarette tobacco at the worn hardwood floor. "I darn near took him out with my pick-up the other night

—just like that other crash, only I stayed on the road. Shoulda ran him over. Man's a menace." He sounded like the guy announcing the Blue Light Special at Q-Mart in Davenport. *Obnoxious.*

Next thing I know, McQuiddy grabbed a three-foot length of PVC pipe and held it like a club. I grabbed his wrist.

"Put that down, *please.*" I gave him my strongest evil-eye.

He set it down and stepped forward. "Did he make it?" All five guys stopped talking and stared at McQuiddy like he'd let one go.

Joshua looked around at the others. "Henry. Yes. I mean, no. I mean, I don't know, Henry. Why'd you want to know?"

"Don't know." The boy's face turned red as a cherry.

"We saw him down by the lake the other day," I said. "Just wondering if he's okay."

"Well, children …" Joshua emphasized the word "children" like we really didn't belong there. "… We'll just have to wait and see if he shows up. He's been spotted in pretty close proximity lately."

"Yeah," Duke added. "He's been real close, too. Like six

inches from the bumper of my truck. Needs to be sent back to the loony bin."

I spotted McQuiddy grabbing for the pipe he'd just put down.

Clank, thunk! That piece of PVC pipe bounced up off the floor and smacked Duke in the shin.

"Shut up, stupid!" McQuiddy squared off like he was getting ready to throw blows.

Stunned silence filled One-Eyed Jack's like the place was being held up at gunpoint. But the gunman was a twelve-year-old boy—McQuiddy.

It took Duke a full five seconds to realize what had happened. A red stain appeared on his jeans at the shin. "Why, you little shit!"

Duke turned and limped toward the boy. His long arms ended at his knees in fists with hairy knuckles. McQuiddy was trapped between plumbing fixtures and toilet seats but, to tell you the truth, he didn't seem to care.

The boy grabbed another piece of PVC pipe and stepped forward, thrusting it in front of him like a sword. I grabbed his arm, but he yanked it away.

Duke laughed with a low, mean snort, like a great ape flashing malicious teeth. He turned to the other boys.

"Look at this little shit. He's loonier than …"

Whump! McQuiddy smashed his other shin.

By now, all the men in the place had formed a semicircle around the pair.

"Aaauuugh!" Duke bellowed. Then he attacked. He grabbed the boy's arm.

McQuiddy went berserk. Kicked Duke's ankle and flailed punches at his stomach and arms. "Eeeeyyaaaaah!" He caught Duke on the chin. "Eeeyyaaah! Eeeyyaaah!" Each of his punches hit something solid.

Duke slung an oversize arm around McQuiddy under his armpit and lifted him like a twig. Big mistake. The boy kicked him hard, in the crotch. Duke howled and tossed the boy like a lit firecracker. The boy hit the hardwood floor banging the back of his head. But not enough to bang any sense into him. He got up, karate-chopped my restraining hand, and charged Duke again. "Orangutan!"

"What!" Duke's face reddened with rage. His orange hair flared out like he'd stuck his finger in a socket. This time, he was ready. Fists tight, knees bent. All those fights I remembered he started, *he* finished. Just as McQuiddy was about to get into a head-on collision with an enraged ape, a large, dark-skinned arm wrapped around his waist.

"Whoa, there, Henry McQuiddy! This is about the worst way to fix this up." Percy Gray wrapped his other arm around the boy's arms for his own personal safety. McQuiddy tried to wriggle free.

"Easy does it there, young man." Percy tightened his grip.

"Let him go." Duke stared with lead-gray eyes. "I'll finish this."

"You won't be finishing nothing, Duke Doreen. You done enough with your mouth." Percy put his broad chest between Duke and McQuiddy as he pushed the boy toward the door. "Nicky, could you catch that door for us, please?"

As I opened the door, Duke turned to Joshua. "Did he just call me a gorilla?"

"Approximately," Joshua replied.

Percy walked us all the way to the trailer park. McQuiddy tried to break free from the big hand on his shoulder a couple of times on the way home.

"I can handle this, Percy. Let me go."

"Right," I said. "In your dreams, McQuiddy."

"Henry McQuiddy, you done wore me out. But you gonna stay with Nicky and me and we *are* gonna get you home."

We walked in silence.

When we got to the trailer park, Percy spoke. He puffed hard between words. "Want me—*puff*—to explain—*puff*—to your mom?"

"Mom?" McQuiddy said. "Why does she need to know anything?"

"McQuiddy," I said. "The back of your head's got a golf ball on it and check out your arm. It's black and blue."

A huge bruise wrapped around McQuiddy's arm where Duke had squeezed it.

"Thanks, Percy. I'll take care of this," McQuiddy said.

I knew McQuiddy's mom was at work and the boy would try to hide all this from her. Tell you the truth, if she were my mom, I'd tell her everything. She's easy to talk to—like my mom used to be.

"You sure is one tough bullhead catfish, Henry McQuiddy." Percy turned to me. "He must be a powerful pain to look after."

"Sure is," I said.

"Say, Nicky Smithers, you don't suppose I could have a word with Henry in private, do you? I know you and he about as close together as mustard on a hotdog."

"I gotta go anyway," Nicky said. "You all right,

McQuiddy?"

"Sure." McQuiddy stared out at the flagpole.

"Try not to do anything else crazy, today. Okay?" The boy wouldn't even look at me.

"See ya," he said.

"Right. See ya. Wouldn't wanna be ya."

I left the two of them leaning against that gray porch rail McQuiddy had painted, wondering if Percy could talk any sense into the boy. The thing is, it wasn't just the Chain Mail Man who put his life on the line for me yesterday. It was this boy. I glanced back one more time and caught McQuiddy watching me.

CHAPTER 13

HENRY

AS NICKY WALKED AWAY, Percy trudged up the steps with me to the trailer's small front porch. He put an elbow on the rail, stuck a toothpick in his mouth, and turned to me. "Orangutan?"

"I don't even know where that came from." I cracked a smile. "Sounded good though, didn't it?"

"Better than *Eeeyyahhh*, I guess." Percy turned away and put both large, dark hands on the porch rail and studied the flagpole monument in the park across the street.

"Percy?"

"Yes, sir?"

"Is there something you wanted to say?"

"Yes, sir." Percy continued his silent gaze.

"Well?"

"Well …" He flipped his toothpick to the other side of his mouth. "That Big Loony stuff. You know anything about that?" His massive, dark face continued to peer forward like a brown, marble statue.

"Not much." I felt the blood rushing to my head. "Can I get a toothpick?"

Percy pulled one out of his shirt pocket. The burst of cinnamon flavor as I stuck it in my mouth seemed to calm me.

"Well, see. Fact is, they say, he was there that night Nicky's mom crashed."

"What?" That hit me like a giant northern pike snapping my fishing line.

"Thought you might want to know." Percy glanced over watching my reaction.

I just chewed real hard on my toothpick. A chilly breeze put goose bumps on my arms as I thought about Nicky.

"Thanks." I stared up at the gray clouds left by that thunderstorm that took Big Loony down the Wapsi.

"You think he made it, Percy? Think he's still alive?"

"Maybe," Percy said.

"Yeah," I repeated. "Maybe."

Percy nodded at the stone base of the flagpole in the center of the park, the one with the decree to the dead Iowa boys. "You know, not all them war casualties show up on a memorial."

"What do you mean?"

"Well there's lots of ways to die." Percy glanced down at me.

"Yeah …" I spit out my toothpick. "Like in a car crash."

The shiny black and white sheriff's car squealed to a stop in front of us. The huge figure of Sheriff Matson lumbered toward us. His broad belly and chest looked like he'd swallowed a beer keg.

"Henry." His wide-brimmed hat hid his beady eyes in shadow, but you could see his jaw bulging with tobacco. "Hear you been tossing merchandise at folks down at One-Eyed-Jack's."

"Maybe." My knees turned to butter.

"Let me give you a little advice, son." He checked the polish on his boots, turned his head, and spat a brown gob right in the middle of the sidewalk. "You're a kid. Got no business meddling in adult affairs. Hear me?" His hateful eyes caught mine.

"I asked you a question, son?"

"Yes, sir. I heard you."

"Good. So Jack decided not to press charges on the damage, but next time, I'll be the one to decide that. Got it?"

"Ycs, sir."

"Good."

As Sheriff Matson left, I noticed that not one time did he ever say anything to or look at Percy.

***

I waited until Saturday morning pancakes to ask. Real maple syrup sweetened the way for tough questions. Every Saturday, *I* made pancakes for both of us like my dad used to. Mom told me that. Even served her breakfast in bed on special occasions like Dad did when she received her promotion to sergeant. Today, she plopped down at the table just as I slid the spatula under the third, golden brown pancake.

I still felt bad about the thing with the chain mail links. I slid the plate of cakes right over the spot where she had shoved the links into the trash with her nightstick. I placed a cup of fresh brewed coffee beside her plate.

"Sleep well?" she asked. "No nightmares?"

I hated that question. It wasn't enough she had to be in all my awake business. She also had to be meddling into my dreams. But I was glad it was the first thing out of her mouth. It meant she knew nothing about the incident at One-Eyed Jack's.

"Not a one," I said.

I waited until the first sweet bite dissolved in her mouth. "Mom?"

"Yes."

"Big Loony. You heard that name?"

Her face turned pale as pancake mix. She didn't look at me. She took a sip of coffee.

"Mom?"

"What?" One hand went to her belt like she was reaching for a weapon.

"Well?"

"Yes," she said. "I've heard of him. Where'd you hear the name?"

"Joshua—down at the hardware store—and Duke Doreen."

"Those guys got nothing better to do than to make a bad thing worse. Thought I told you to stay away from them."

"Mom. It's the *only* place in town to get minnows. So here's my real question. Did you know about him being there that night Nicky's mom crashed?"

She set down her cup, now clenching it in both hands. "Yes."

"Did he cause the accident?"

"No one knows. My police report said he was there, that's all. Nicky's dad sure as shootin' thinks he did." She stared at her coffee quivering in the morning sunlight.

"You saw him there?" I asked.

"When I arrived at the scene, he was trying to pry open a door to get her out. But it was already too late."

I wanted so badly to tell her that this guy was the man who saved Nicky's life. I bit my lip. "Who is he, Mom?"

"He's, he's a guy released from the mental hospital up in Independence. I suppose that's why they call him that," she said.

Did she think she raised a stupid kid? What was she hiding? Is he my dad? I decided to let her off the hook for now. I needed to tell Nicky the latest update.

"Yeah, well, those guys don't know what they're talking about," I said.

"That's right," Mom agreed.

***

I waited until my mom finished her pancakes and coffee, read her morning paper, and went out to check the mail. It came early on Saturdays. All the mailboxes for the trailers stood watch at the entrance to our park, a good distance from our trailer. I grabbed the phone as soon as she went out the door.

"Nicky?"

"Yes."

"That man, that Chain Mail Man?"

"Yes?" she said.

"The one who saved your life?"

"McQuiddy! I know who you mean. Just spit it out."

"Well, I found out he was there that night?" I said.

"What night?"

"That night, you know, when your mom had her, you know …"

I could just make out her breathing on the other end of the line. I waited.

"You sure?"

"My mom went to the scene and found him there. It's in her report."

I could hear Nicky's heavy breaths in the phone silence.

"Dianna was right," I said. "It was a man, not a deer."

More breaths.

"You okay, Nicky?"

"Sure."

"You surc?" I askcd.

"I said so, didn't I? Look, I gotta go. Bye."

"Bye, Nicky." She's about as close to "okay" as Australia.

CHAPTER 14

NICKY

IF MCQUIDDY ONLY KNEW the rest of it … . I slammed a flyswatter on a big old green fly buzzing on the window. *SPLAT!*

CHAPTER 15

HENRY

SATURDAY AFTERNOON, NICKY WASN'T Nicky. I didn't get to see her or talk to her until the softball game. I had tried to call her three times. When I spotted her standing out by third base, I barely recognized her. Her spunk was gone—and her gum. I figured the news about Big Loony and her mom's accident must have hit her pretty hard. I wondered what else her dad might have added to the story.

She stood there next to third base, arms folded, her glove tucked under her opposite arm, propped mostly on one leg, like she was just waiting for the corn to grow. She stared at the first batter like a zombie.

Late afternoon on a Saturday in McGrawsland, a

softball game was *the* town event. Everybody was there, even Professor Joshua Graham Bell and his buddies from One-Eyed Jack's. Nicky's dad sat directly behind the Lady Catfish dugout. Mom moved us to sit behind the backstop, as far away as possible from Mr. Smithers. She kept trying to put a hand on my shoulder, which I skillfully kept squirming out of. She smelled of almond shampoo and wore a white cotton dress with tiny red roses. It reminded me of Nicky's lost rose tattoo.

The first batter popped out to Blanche, the pitcher. Blanche snagged the ball, held her glove to her chest, turned her blond-haired, blue-eyed, *Cosmopolitan*-cover face right at me, and winked! I felt my cheeks burn. To make matters worse, Mom spotted the wink and elbowed me. *So embarrassing.*

Clack! The sound of an aluminum can being crushed turned my head. Out by the trash can alongside the third base bleachers, grimy hands grasped that smashing device. *Clack!* It came down on another soda can and flattened it.

From a thicket of dirty hair, his blue eyes glanced over at Nicky. Like the chain link fence that separated them, his chest was covered with links of chain mail. His camouflage U.S. Army field jacket was torn at the sleeve and his forehead had a pretty bad cut on it. *Lots of snags in that river.*

"Nicky!" I hollered.

She didn't look up, just stared at the batter.

"Nicky!"

She turned her head away, folding her arms across her chest.

"Nicky! On your right!"

She shook her head, then slowly turned and looked over her shoulder.

The trouble was, everybody in McGrawsland heard me. Even Duke Doreen.

"That's it!" Duke grabbed a bat and headed through the bleachers to the man he called Big Loony.

I shot out of the stands and took a shortcut through the playing field. I caught up with Nicky heading for the fence.

"Leave him alone!" Nicky hollered.

"Stupid dogfish." I called Duke the name of my most despised trash fish. I passed Nicky, threw myself at the chain link fence, and latched onto the eight-foot fence like Spider-Man. But I didn't have Spider-Man's sticky stuff. My foot missed a hold and I slid to the ground with a thud.

"Get the hell out of here, ya' big loony!" Duke

lumbered toward him wielding the bat on one shoulder.

Big Loony froze like a possum caught in the beams of headlights, pretending not to be there—or anywhere.

Duke raised the bat.

"Leave him alone!" Nicky hollered.

The man shielded his face with an arm.

"You hear me?" Duke stuck the bat in the air like an exclamation point.

Taking a step back, Big Loony's eyes shifted left and right looking for a way out. He bent over and started to pick up three smashed aluminum cans.

As he did that, the bat came down and thwacked his shoulder knocking him face first into the black Iowa dirt. Duke was poised to deliver another blow. He swung.

The blur of the bat stopped three inches from Big Loony's neck.

"Guess you need to turn up that hearing aid, Duke." Nicky's dad caught the bat with one hand and turned Duke's wrist with the other. Duke's face twisted in pain as he let go of the bat and dropped to his knees. "She said to leave him alone." He nodded at his daughter.

Big Loony groaned as he pushed himself with up his arms. He stuck the cans in a side pocket of his green backpack and turned to leave, glancing back at the crowd with a mud-smeared face. His eyes dashed from face to face in the crowd and finally fixed on Mom. I caught it. Their eyes met. Something like lightning jumped between those two dark clouds. Just seconds. Mom buried her face in her hands. I had to swallow hard to keep from crying myself, and I wasn't even sure why.

Then he bolted. I noticed his weird way of running. He kept his head down as he ran as if he were dodging bullets, or mortar blasts, cutting back and forth, zigzagging the soybean field, headed for the Wapsi.

I watched Nicky's dad lift Duke by the armpit with one muscular arm and say something to him that only Duke could hear. Duke backed away.

Mr. Smithers nodded at Nicky, then turned and looked into the stands. For the first time I could ever remember, I saw Nicky's dad and my mom look at each other for more than a split second and with no malice in their eyes. Mom's were blurred with tears.

I put a hand on Nicky's shoulder watching her try to fight back her tears.

"You okay?" The stupidest question I had ever asked anyone.

"I miss her."

"Yeah. Me too." I really liked Nicky's mom. Used to be okay to go to Nicky's trailer when her mom was around. I remembered her face better than my own dad's.

Nicky's dad came up and the girl buried her face in his chest.

I returned to the stands, sat by my mom, and put my arm around her.

Chapter 16

NICKY

THE PHONE WEIGHED A thousand pounds as I picked it up to call McQuiddy that night. He'd called me about ten times that day. Just wasn't ready. Now, with all that commotion at the softball game, I had to tell him. He wasn't the only one who'd found something out about the chain mail guy.

I knew why Dad had carried all that anger on his shoulders for the last four years.

"Hello."

"It's Nicky."

"About time you called back," McQuiddy said. "You all right?"

"You?" I asked back.

"Not really."

The boy must have been bleeding to give that answer.

"McQuiddy?" I hated this. Like punching a guy when he's already down.

"Yeah?"

"Big Loony? The Chain Mail Man? When he lifted me out of that river? His arm …" I stopped.

"Spit it out, Nicky."

"There's a tattoo on it, a real one."

I could hear his breathing stop.

"Three hearts linked together. Below it, the words, *NO MATTER WHAT.*"

CHAPTER 17

HENRY

THAT HIT ME IN the gut, worse than any blow Duke Doreen could ever throw. But I'm glad it was Nicky. It softened it a little.

I couldn't sleep that night. For one thing it was the last night of summer vacation. Junior high school started tomorrow. For another, I just couldn't get him off my mind, that look he gave Mom, the way he ran like a soldier under attack. And finally, Mom was awake most of the night, too. I heard her in the front room, talking.

I crept out of bed and tiptoed to the edge of the entrance. A candle reflected in her teary eyes.

She spoke to a picture. "It's hard. It's really hard seeing you like that."

Was she talking to Dad?

She got up. I snuck back to bed and pulled the covers over my head. I heard her open my bedroom door. She stood in the doorway for a long time.

"I'm sorry, Henry," she whispered and closed the door. My eyes got hot. She didn't need to apologize. She's the one who stayed.

I stared at the army of stars out my window and finally dozed off. An hour later, a recurring nightmare jarred me awake. *I'm fishing in the Wapsi and someone whispers, "snags," and a giant shadow comes over me.* I bolted upright. Out my window, a three-quarter moon turned the broad leaves of the cornfield into silver blades, the swords of a thousand knights in a crusade. My stomach ached—like one of those blades had stabbed me.

Found it. The light gleamed off the shiny surface—the photo I gave Mom from that letter—my dad holding me upside down by one arm. He had the biggest grin on his face. Mom had taken the picture. I stuck it in my T-shirt pocket.

Nothing else mattered. I had to meet him. Pulling on my black T-shirt and jeans and grabbing my tennis shoes, I crept into the front room. Sliding open her desk drawer, I took out the tiny flashlight and switched it on.

On the porch steps, I put on my shoes. The fireflies were thick, blinking like those yellow warning lights at an accident. I could think of only one place to look. I hopped on my bike.

***

The planks of the bridge were damp but not slick. A three-quarter moon created a bluish path of light in front of me. Shadow lines from the posts on the side of the bridge fluttered by as my bike clacked across the boards. Dad would hear me coming for sure.

I slid down the trail that led under the bridge, careful to avoid the sticker bushes. The moon brushed a circle of streaming, silver light onto the river. The light from the reflection danced like pale-blue Indian ghosts on the beams underneath the bridge. The dirt bank gradually slanted downward from the bridge twenty feet to the swirling water.

Nobody there. I crawled under the four-foot clearance.

I clicked on my flashlight. Beside the remains of a campfire lay a couple sheets of cardboard box. I knelt down and patted the ashes. Cold. I raked my fingers through the powdery stuff. My forefinger poked through a loop, and I lifted out three aluminum pop-tops linked together.

Above the campfire, the blue moonlight outlined a bulky object tucked under the bridge, creating a shadow behind it. Turning my light on it, I spotted a camouflage backpack lying face up.

Sticking my flashlight in my mouth, I crawled up to it on my elbows. Opening the flap, I carefully pulled out each item: three pairs of socks, a pair of dirty jeans, a tightly folded, clear plastic poncho, and Mom's cobalt-blue scarf. I remembered her asking about it that day we found those flowers on the porch. I buried my face in it and took a deep whiff. I could smell the almonds.

A wave of pain washed over me. *That's all he has left of her, a scarf.*

I felt tears, remembering when I almost lost Nicky. She thought I was crying about my dad. Now, I was. I wiped my face with the scarf.

"Mine," a deep voice said.

"Mmmmph!" The flashlight in my mouth muffled my shout. He hunched down making his way under the bridge.

"Mine." The shadow held out a hand.

I pulled the flashlight out of my mouth, with my hand

trembling, holding up the scarf. "Do you know who I am?"

"Maybe." He snatched the scarf.

I pulled the picture out of my pocket. With trembling hands, I offered it to him.

A huge, grimy hand held it between thumb and forefinger while I shined the light on it.

"That's me." I pointed at the little boy.

He looked confused. His blue eyes glistened.

I pointed at the man in the picture. "And that's you."

He looked frightened, like a wild animal caught in headlights. He didn't move. He didn't speak.

"You want it?" I nodded at the photo.

His nod *yes* was little more than a blink.

"It's yours," I said.

Without a word, he carefully placed it in an inside pocket of the backpack. Gathering his clothing and the scarf, he stuffed them back in, not looking at me. He secured the pack on his back and turned away. I shined the light on his aluminum chain mail vest.

"Wait." I pointed the light at my own face. "You know me, right?"

He glanced at my face and pointed to the moonlit river. A sandbar collected the logs, branches, and debris creating a silhouette of what looked like the shape of a three-headed dragon. It quivered in the gentle current.

He nodded at that dragon. "Lots of snags."

The scene came crashing in on me. My recurring dream. The shadow was my dad. He had taken me fishing, here, under this very bridge. I had hung up my line and he held my pole, working it free. *Lots of snags,* he'd said.

I had a hundred more questions. "Dad?"

The Chain Mail Man crawled away.

"Wait, Dad." I turned the flashlight on him.

He turned, touched his hand to his forehead, and gave me a short, salute-like wave with a brief glance. His forehead creased with pain and his eyes glistened. His jaws bulged. My light hit his arm. I spotted the tattoo of three hearts and the words, *NO MATTER WHAT.* He'd kept his promise. He came back—at least what was left of him.

That salute of his was like a knight raising the visor of his helmet to show he was friend not foe, like Lancelot. More than a friend—my dad.

I tried to follow him, but he took a route toward the backwaters where the muck was deep and the serpents were busy. I watched the chain mail on my dad's broad back shimmer in the moonlight as he disappeared into the thick woods on the other side of the bridge.

I turned back and knelt at the cold campfire. I fished the three linked pieces of chain mail out of the ashes, pulled out my green coin purse, and squeezed it open. Blowing the ash-dust off the aluminum rings, I dropped them in.

The first ray of sunlight hit the top of McGrawsland Bridge as my bike pounded on the loose boards like the hooves of the steed of a lone knight riding home from battle, Sir Galahad, son of Lancelot. I declared myself victorious. I had found my dad, still alive. Maybe still on a quest. Maybe slaying dragons inside his head. Definitely rescuing damsels in distress.

I wore those thoughts like armor. But a big gash had been slashed into my breastplate near my heart. That's where the pain throbbed and that's when I saw Nicky.

She waited for me at the other end of the bridge on her bike, the rising sun highlighting her burnt orange hair and freckled face.

"Saw you leave," she said. "Making sure you didn't jump into that river again."

"He's my dad," I said.

"Told you."

Chapter 18

NICKY

"THOSE POLICE LIGHTS UP ahead?" I asked McQuiddy as we rode home from the bridge.

"Now I'm in for it." He hopped off his bike and walked it toward the scene ahead.

Sgt. Doris McQuiddy's squad car was parked crosswise on the gravel causeway where the lake emptied through the culvert into the marsh. The sheriff's car blocked the other causeway entrance. A tow truck sat in the middle feeding out its steel cable to a deputy at the marsh-side of the road. Spotlights from the two squad cars focused on the truck cable.

"Mom?" In the flashing lights, McQuiddy's face turned blue and red and blue and red. The morning breeze lifted some of his sandy hair straight up.

"What in the hell are you doing out here this time of night, mister?"

"Hey, Mrs. McQuiddy." I tried to deflect the bomb that she was about to explode.

"Nicky? Thought you'd have more sense than this one."

She turned back to her prime target … her son. "What in the Sam Hill are you doing here?"

"Went for a moonlight ride." He nodded at the moon for support. "What are you doing here?" he asked.

"My dang job!" his mom said. "You two need to back way off. This is a crime scene."

"What crime?" McQuiddy asked.

"Police business." His mom pulled out her walkie. "And none of yours. Now go." She turned away and started talking cop-code into her device.

We backed up our bikes but not so much that we couldn't see the action. The winch started groaning as the tow truck lifted its cargo.

I expected to see some old pickup truck that had gone over the edge with a drunk driver. Instead, just a limp body came up, a man in blue jeans and a yellow shirt, and, *holy-moly*, one chartreuse tennis shoe.

That's when I noticed the other shoe sitting on the edge of the causeway with an evidence marker beside it.

The body dangled above the road, slowly rotating around in its canvas-belted harness. It was one of those scenes you never forget, like the one of my mom's car wrapped around that tree.

Terrence's head was dented on one side. I felt McQuiddy's elbow nudge my arm.

"I know the big ape who did this," McQuiddy said.

"Not for sure, you don't," I said.

The sheriff's deputy slushed his way out of the mucky marsh hoisting a long pole above his head. At one end a cylinder was covered with a mass of pondweed. When he got up to the road, he tamped the weeds off. The can crusher.

"Take that to Davenport," the sheriff said. "Examine the blood. Get prints."

I glanced at McQuiddy. The boy looked lost, completely lost.

"No way," he said.

Chapter 19

HENRY

FOR THE NEXT TWO months the primary subject of conversation at One-Eyed Jack's was about how Big Loony must have murdered Terrence Ashton. For two months, Mom told me nothing about the investigation. For two months, neither Nicky nor I saw any signs of my dad in his chain mail vest. Even if they caught him, most people figured they'd just put him back in the loony bin where he belonged. That's what the sheriff reported in response to the criticism that he hadn't caught his man.

I had a different theory. I believed Duke Doreen got hold of Dad's can crusher and went after Terrence. Terrence was the one who saw Duke pull a knife on me. Dad didn't even have his can crusher that night. I know. I saw him under the bridge.

Mom let me go with her to Davenport on police business so I could visit Percy. I just couldn't hold it in.

"It wasn't Dad, Mom. It was Duke Doreen."

"Listen to me, Henry." Mom laid her free hand on the evidence bag containing a bundle wrapped in brown butcher paper and tied up with heavy twine. "This is *my* job, not yours. I can't be talking to you or anybody about the case. Please. Keep your theories to yourself."

"But Mom. I saw Dad that night and he didn't have his can crusher."

"I know. Henry, please. Leave it alone. No more talk about the case."

She knows?

We pulled into the Davenport Police Department parking lot, which was just a few blocks from the levee.

Mr. Smithers stood in the walkway to the rear entrance waving at Mom.

Sgt. McQuiddy closed her eyes a moment. "God, everyone thinks they're a detective."

Mom opened her door. "Don't touch that evidence package, Henry. Somehow, I've got to get it past snooping eyes." She nodded at Mr. Smithers.

"You know he's going to come after you if this falls apart," Mr. Smithers said.

"I know." She took his arm and guided him to his car. "Please, Richard. Let me do my job."

While she was putting Mr. Smithers in his car, I couldn't resist. I turned the package in my hands. I found a corner of the package slipping open under the twine. A khaki piece of an article of clothing had a spot of blood on it. *Is that Dad's army shirt?* I really needed some time to wrap my head around all this.

I tucked the corner in and set it back the way I found it.

***

Percy and I both leaned on the rail that held his two fishing poles. We stared out at the Mississippi as we talked. The river cleared up a bit in the fall chill, from a mud gray to a murky blue on a sunny day. Percy set his poles in front of the old baseball stadium. We had a green wall behind us. I wondered how many homers made it over that wall and into the river.

"So see, I thought it wasn't my dad who killed him. I thought it was Duke. But I saw something a while ago that makes me not so sure."

Percy just nodded and changed the subject. "Sure is

getting chilly." He pushed his maroon wool scarf down the front of his jacket. Breath-smoke puffed from his mouth. Not many good fishing days left.

I studied Percy's face. "What happened to him, Percy? What made him like that?"

"Can only speculate."

"Go ahead." I watched his eyes. They looked up and away, like he was trying to find something lost, something hiding in his brain somewhere.

"I suspect something real bad happened to him back there. Heard he was one of them POWs for a while, you know, prisoners of war."

"POW?" Saying it made it real for me.

Percy nodded.

I pulled out my green coin purse, squeezed it open, pulled out the three links of chain mail, and stuck them in my pocket. I slipped out the yellow square of paper, unfolded it, and handed it to Percy. "What do you make of this?" I pointed at the word "manacles."

Percy's eyebrows rose. "Yes. I did hear tell of something about that. I heard a story that Viet Cong had these rough metal bracelets and chains and all. Might have been something like that."

"Yeah, maybe." I reread the note for the hundredth time.

"But didn't you say you got this note a few months ago?"

"Yes." I said.

"Well, he was a prisoner five or six years ago. Got rescued and let out of the army about four years ago," Percy said.

"Maybe he was just remembering or having a flashback or something," I offered.

"Maybe." Percy stared out at the Mississippi.

"What happened, Percy? Why didn't he come home?"

"Can only speculate." Percy looked down at me.

"Go ahead," I said. "Speculate."

"Well, truth is, he did *try* to come home for a spell. Nobody could hardly recognize him though. He'd just wander about town. Never even tried knocking on his own door. Went sneaking around looking like a shadow of a man. My Martha fixed him up with some vittles once in a while, leaving them on the porch. They were always gone by the next day. I figure he left the best part of himself back there in that war. Then, after the accident, he just disappeared again."

"You mean the one with Nicky's mom?"

Percy nodded. "Like I said before, about casualties and that memorial."

I finally understood. Some of the casualties didn't die in the war. They died later, inside themselves—like my dad.

"It's just that they ain't held no funeral for some of them other casualties." Percy stared across the river. I was pretty sure he was remembering his wife's funeral. "Sometimes I think you just gotta sort of hold your own funeral, a private one. To end all the *what ifs,* if you know what I mean."

"Yep," I said. "I think I do."

A bell rattled furiously.

I watched the tip of Percy's fishing pole bend.

He grabbed the line and yanked. "Got him!"

CHAPTER 20

NICKY

I LIKED HER. MCQUIDDY'S mom. Since we were now allowed in each other's homes, I got to know her better. She was a lot cooler than the boy let on. But then, what can you expect from a boy like McQuiddy? He made things up, like homemade stink bait for catfish, and his lies smelled just as bad.

I heard things from Mrs. McQuiddy, not so much about the murder investigation but more about the past. She asked me to call her Doris, at least when McQuiddy wasn't around and she wasn't in uniform. I heard things about my mom I'd never heard before. Turns out they were, what she called, "baby buggy buddies." Used to push McQuiddy and me over to the Busy Bea together every Wednesday for the lunch special, homemade split pea soup with ham hocks. Said she and Mom were always trading clothes. They liked each other's taste.

Seems like Sgt. Doris McQuiddy spent most Saturdays away. She'd leave early in the morning and return late at night. Said she was going away on business. But when she stopped wearing her uniform and started wearing dresses on those Saturdays, I wondered if she had found a new gentleman friend.

I worried about the boy. He'd just stare into space when I'd ask him if he wanted to go fishing. Maybe it was the basketball. He was already six-foot-two in seventh grade. He obsessed with practice, by himself, like he was in boot camp or something. There was this drill sergeant inside his head pushing him. I saw him making himself do pushups because he missed a free throw.

McQuiddy's mom had just driven away in her El Camino one Saturday. I spotted her from the picnic bench in the park. Two of my teammates on the seventh-grade girls' volleyball team and I hung out there. The paint all flaking off the bench, we had to watch for splinters.

"Here he comes." Blanche had developed a defective aspect to her otherwise *perfect girl* image. She had a *thing* for boys, McQuiddy in particular. The boy was oblivious.

McQuiddy came down his porch steps with a basketball pinned on his hip with one hand and a can of pop in his other. The months had put some meat on the boy's bones, but his bright orange T-shirt still hung loosely on his shoulders. Still, he'd gained two notches on his belt.

When he hit the street, he dribbled his well-worn basketball, probably headed for the school outdoor courts.

As he came closer, I spotted something weird. That khaki army belt he used for tying things to his bike was now wrapped around his head like a bandana. The shiny brass buckle gleamed off his forehead.

"Hey, Henry." Blanche waved him over.

"What's up?" the boy asked.

"The sky. What's that for?" Blanche pointed at the belt on his forehead and elbowed Gertrude.

"Funeral," he said.

A black permanent marker stuck out his T-shirt pocket.

"What?" Gertrude asked.

"You heard me."

"Right." Blanche rolled her eyes at Gertrude. "Say, Henry, you going to play on the team? I hear you're really good." Her big blue eyes searched his face for a reaction.

"Maybe." He looked down at his khaki shoelaces with a red face.

"Hope so." I swear she almost batted her eyes.

McQuiddy shot a question mark my way. I knew what it meant, *What's up with this girl?*

I shrugged my shoulders.

"I'll be sitting in the front row if you play, Henry." She enjoyed watching him squirm.

"Shut up, Blanche," I said.

"Wait," Blanche said. "I got something for you, Henry. A present." She reached into her blue jean back pocket and pulled out a circular, yellow patch with a black horse head.

"Got it at the army surplus store in Davenport. Mom says it was your dad's unit." She gave him her shiny, pink lipstick smile.

He stared down at the patch like a zombie.

"I'm sorry about … you know … your dad," she said.

McQuiddy's face turned gray as gravel. "Thank you." He looked up. "But no thank you." He raised his eyebrows at me and turned away, robot-like, basketball on his hip, soda in hand.

He faced the McGrawsland Memorial Park flagpole, the tallest between two rivers, the memorial to Iowa soldiers killed in the war. He chugged the rest of his pop, stared straight ahead, and marched forward.

Chapter 21

HENRY

"SEE YOU AROUND, HENRY," Blanche hollered.

I ignored her. Nicky didn't.

"Shut *up*, Blanche!"

"I'm just saying *bye*, okay?"

I marched away from them, clear about my mission.

I passed a trash can about ten feet away on my left. I crushed my pop can and shot a hook shot. *Swish!* A weird thought came over me: *I should have saved the pop-top.*

Ready, halt, one-two … I marched to a stop in front of the roster on the concrete base of the flagpole. I read the names of every single Iowan casualty of the Vietnam war before I pulled out my permanent marker and laid it on top of the Plexiglas cover. *He's still not there.*

Crouching in front of the window that protected the list, I laid the three pop-tops linked together to make chain mail on the grass in front. My dad's attempt to protect himself. I took my surplus army belt from my forehead and spread it out in front, just below the three links.

I pulled out the felt box bulging in my pocket and opened it. The Bronze Star gleamed in the autumn sun. *Dad, you're a hero. You're my hero—no matter what.* I closed the box and crammed it back in my pocket.

I dropped to both knees in front of the Plexiglas.

With a steady, serious hand, I began printing in large block letters, putting all my attention into making sure the lines were straight and true. I stood and said the only words I could think of.

"God bless you, Dad."

About-face! I marched away from the monument. A new name had appeared.

Sgt. Lance McQuiddy

***

News of the additional name on the memorial took less than an hour to reach my mom at work. Sheriff Matson told her she needed to control her son. Mom was so furious she didn't speak. She just stalked around the trailer like a mad woman.

The next Saturday morning, under the sheriff's orders, I found out that permanent does not mean permanent. I refer to the permanent black marker I used. A solvent that smelled like toxic chemicals, a soft cloth, and rubber gloves were waiting for me at the monument.

The worst part was Sheriff Matson decided to put park maintenance man Duke Doreen in charge of me for the removal.

"Now you did it." He was, thankfully, brief. He folded his arms across his chest. I began wiping away my dad's name. But I couldn't wipe away those blue eyes gleaming at me under that bridge. *Was he crying?* I couldn't wipe away the ache in my guts. I couldn't wipe away what Percy had said about the *casualties* of that war. As far as I could figure, my dad was another casualty.

Duke just stood there, so close I could smell the tobacco smoke on him. He was so quiet. Creepy-like.

"Least you got to see him," he blurted.

I just about swallowed my spearmint gum, baffled by his words.

"Your dad. You saw him."

"So?" I looked up at Duke. His eyes looked weird, like a

baby bird's, kind of bulgy.

"So, I never met mine," Duke said.

I didn't understand his words. "Who'd you never meet?" I finished wiping off Dad's name.

"My dad." He jerked his head away. "Ever."

"Sorry, man," I said.

"It's all right. Mom said he was a bum anyway." Duke glanced over at me. "I guess I'm sorry, too."

That's when I figured out who he was really swinging that baseball bat at during that softball game. He wasn't swinging at my dad. He was swinging at his. He probably figured that they were both deserters—of their families.

I got that. But what I didn't get was the whole other thing. What about Terrence?

"Did you kill him?" I asked.

"Your dad? No. No way."

"Not my dad," I said. "Terrence."

"Terrence?"

"You forget his name?"

"Not ever, McQuiddy. Terrence was the only guy in this whole town who treated me like a human being. He'd always have a spare leftover donut from Bea's to give me. Always a kind word. When I'd finish my coffee and head for work, he'd always say …" Duke took a couple of deep breaths on account of he was tearing up. "He'd say, 'You hang in there, Duke, and have a good one.' Every morning."

Now I was really mad. Mad at myself. *See what happens when you jump to conclusions.*

"Sorry, Duke. I'm an idiot."

"It's okay. Truth is, Terrence chewed me out for calling your dad that name. Said I had no respect for a guy who fought in the war. Shamed me."

"Dad's one of them." I pointed at the names on the monument.

Duke nodded. "Yeah."

Everybody who passed by watched us. I could tell I was the new town freak. The weird kid. The crazy kid. Like my dad. But he's not a murderer. No way.

On Monday, I walked through school like *I* was the Chain Mail Man, staring straight ahead. Pretending not to notice the giggles of girls. Pretending not to notice boys turning their heads away quickly so as not to be caught staring at me. Pretending not to notice teachers making exceptions for me in class. "Henry, you take as long as you need to finish this." Pretending not to notice the empty seats on each side of me in the lunch room. Trying to pretend not to hear Nicky sitting right across from me, talking to me.

CHAPTER 22

NICKY

YOU KNOW, MCQUIDDY'S DEALT with his dad being nuts, maybe a murderer, maybe dead. He's dealt with being embarrassed in front of the whole dang town when he tried to put it all to rest with his little ceremony. He's dealt with his mom being ready to put him up for adoption. With all of that, you'd think, *Can't this boy catch a break?*

So when Sheriff Matson showed up in our fifth-period algebra class with a set of cuffs asking for Henry McQuiddy, I got my answer to the catching-a-break question. *No.*

"Son, is this yours?" He held up a large baggie of what I guessed was marijuana, at least I think that's what it was. Truth is, I've never seen marijuana except on TV, and I doubt if McQuiddy had either.

"What the ...?" McQuiddy stood and glanced over at me. The boy didn't even know what he was supposed to do.

"Stand right here, son, and turn around. We found this in your locker."

"What is it?" McQuiddy asked.

"Oh, come on, boy. You know very well what this is. We found some of this in your Dad's backpack, too. You been smoking dope with your daddy, boy? Huh? Under the old McGrawsland Bridge?

"My dad hates drugs. He'd never ..." The cuffs clicked on McQuiddy's wrists. "Ouch!"

Leave him alone!" I jumped out of my chair and charged, aiming for the sheriff's largest target—his belly. I bashed my head into his beer gut and bounced off like a ping-pong ball. I was ready to have his deputy put cuffs on me as well, then I realized there was no deputy. Matson was here all by his big-bag-of-wind self.

"I'll deal with you later, young lady. Right now, this boy is going to jail." He pushed me aside with one of his big ham-size arms.

Worst part? As I looked around the classroom for support from our classmates, every face had the same look, a look that said *This boy's been doing dope with his crazy, murdering dad.*

The boy had his military look on. He just stared out the window. He might be taken prisoner. But he'd never talk. Like his dad. Just name, rank, and serial number.

That's when I saw something I will picture in my mind over and over again because it makes me feel so dang good. Sheriff Matson buckled and dropped like a circus elephant going down on its front legs.

A police baton had clipped him at the back of the knees, and Sgt. Doris McQuiddy grabbed the sheriff's arms, jerked them behind his back, and put handcuffs on his thick wrists. The deputy stood behind her with his gun drawn.

"Sheriff Matson, I am arresting you for the murder of Terrence Ashton. You have the right to remain silent. Anything you say now may be used against you in a court of law."

"Bitch!"

"You ever try to cuff my kid again, and you'll see just what a bitch I can be."

All right, Doris McQuiddy! I'd never heard her talk like that, but it sure did sound good in that moment.

"And your son's a son of a ..." He stopped when she

shoved her police baton in front of his face.

"I'm sure the judge will want to know all that." She returned to her "all business" approach. "Take him away, Corporal." The deputy seemed to enjoy squeezing the arm of the windbag so hard that he winced.

"You all should be thanking me instead of cuffing me," the sheriff said. "Got rid of two deviants with one blow."

"Yeah, and one of them happened to be my husband," Sgt. McQuiddy said and just turned away.

She went over to her son, took off his handcuffs, and did something no junior high school boy ever wants to have happen at school, especially not in front of classmates—even more embarrassing than the whole marijuana bust. His mom hugged him.

Next to my own mom, I gotta say, *Mrs. McQuiddy's my new role model. She shut down the sheriff.*

CHAPTER 23

HENRY

"YOU KNEW IT WASN'T Dad, didn't you, Mom?"

"Yes, Henry, I knew." She pulled off her police belt with all its gear on it, hung it on a hook, and flopped into a chair at the kitchen table, letting out a puff of air.

"Sorry, Mom."

"For what?"

"For being such a pain about him."

"Sorry for the slap."

"How did you find out about the sheriff?"

"We're done here, Henry. Can't say a thing to you about it and don't start giving me your theories. This has to be done by the book. You understand?"

"I get it."

I knew that the only place she'd talk about any of this was in the courtroom.

Nicky and I snuck in the back of the gallery and hunkered down in our chairs so Mom couldn't see me. Nicky's dad had brought us to Davenport for the trial. The courtroom smelled faintly like an old ashtray. The gray, cloth seats sunk in the center from overuse. The dim lights, plus the light slipping in from the high windows, illuminated dust particles wandering in the air like lost souls.

"Is it true, Sheriff Matson, that you heard that Terrence Ashton was moving to Davenport to live with your son?" Michael Stamper, the assistant district attorney prosecuting the case, turned to the jury placing one hand on the lapel of his gray, tweed suit. The guy was tall and skinny, like me, but his thin, pale face and fancy fingernails told me he spent most of his time indoors.

I elbowed Nicky with a grin when I spotted Percy in the back row of the jury panel. I bet Nicky's dad had something to do with making sure the jury was *balanced.* The Civil Liberties Union that he worked for really pushed for mixed juries.

"No." The sheriff looked away like it was a waste of his

time to be here.

Terrence's mom had died. Terrence always told Nicky and me that when she did, he and Norman, the sheriff's son, planned to move in together in Davenport. Now that I was in junior high, I knew what that *together* meant.

"Did you recently pull over Terrence in his car for a traffic violation?"

"No."

"Then you had no reason to visit Terrence—in his car?"

"No." The Sheriff raised his eyebrows.

"Sheriff, do you remember what you said about Terrence and Lance McQuiddy on the day you were arrested?"

"Objection! No foundation."

"Sheriff, did you say at that time that you 'got rid of two deviants with one blow'?"

"Objection."

"Overruled," the judge said.

"No," the sheriff replied.

"Oh, then I guess you don't remember calling the arresting officer a 'bitch' either."

"Objection."

"Sustained."

"Thank you, Sheriff." Prosecutor Stamper sat.

The defense attorney rose wearing a three-piece dark suit that fit like a glove. Just a slight hint of a sarcastic smile crossed the big lips of his rounded face. His head donned a crop of white hair that looked like he belonged in a hair commercial. Very distinguished. Only his name seemed imperfect for the job, *Mr. Joseph Gander.* Wondered if he had a cousin named *Miss Goose.* We'd heard he flew in from Chicago.

"Sheriff, let's get to the point. Isn't it true that you came upon the murder scene as a result of finding one of the victim's shoes on the side of the road?" The defense attorney placed the chartreuse shoe on an evidence table in the front of the courtroom and walked over to the jury, looking at just the front row, all what the sheriff would call *good old boys.* Jurors one through six were picked by Gander. Percy sat in the back row with jurors seven through twelve.

"Yes."

"Were your clothes wet?"

"No."

"And where was the body found?"

"Back in the swamp below the causeway."

"And isn't it true that swamp is a couple of feet deep in water and muck?"

"Yes."

"And yet your clothes were as dry as a bone."

"Yes," the sheriff glanced at my mom. "Dry as a bone."

"Thank you, Sheriff." Defense attorney Gander gave a quick smile to the jury and sat.

"Redirect, your honor?" Prosecutor Stamper stood.

"Yes."

"Sheriff Matson, was the time of death of the victim approximately three to five a.m. according to the coroner's report?"

"Yes."

"And your report shows that you found the body around seven a.m.?"

"Yes."

"How long does it take you to change into dry clothes?"

"Objection."

"Sustained."

"No further questions, your honor."

***

With Mom's back to us in the courtroom there was no problem with us staying out of sight. But then she was called as a witness. From up on the stand, she spotted us and gave me the look of doom.

"Sgt. McQuiddy, what first led you to determine that the sheriff was a suspect?"

"I, um, interviewed Lance McQuiddy."

What the heck, Mom! You've been talking to Dad? You found him? He's alive? Nicky squeezed my arm hard.

"But isn't it true that Lance McQuiddy is a mental patient at Independence Hospital?"

"Yes."

"How could you rely on the words of a mental patient?"

"I didn't. I backed up his words with evidence."

"Objection!" the defense attorney hollered.

"Overruled."

My mind was still spinning from the Independence Hospital thing. They put only really crazy people in there. I mean like screaming, spitting, tearing-your-hair-out crazy people. Not my dad.

"I'd like to draw your attention to Exhibit 6, this shirt you found in the things belonging to Lance McQuiddy. How can you be certain that this is his shirt?"

"Well, I, and various townspeople had seen him wearing

it during his several appearances in town. That's a Fifth Army patch."

She pointed at the horse head patch on the shoulder. "His unit. And those are his sergeant stripes. And I found this in his closet at Independence Hospital."

"Are these bloodstains on the sleeve?"

"Yes."

"And do you have evidence about those stains?

"Yes. DNA testing shows that the stains are from Sheriff Matson's blood."

"When you brought in the sheriff, did you find any wounds on his body?"

"He had a cut on his wrist."

"Can you describe the cut?"

"Yes, it was about an inch-long wound, not very deep." She pointed to her own wrist to show where it was.

"Like a wound you would get if you cut yourself with a sharp instrument?" Prosecutor Stamper looked at the jury like he wanted them to pay attention to this next part.

"Yes."

"Objection."

"Sustained."

"I draw your attention to Exhibit 7." The prosecutor

lifted the chain mail vest out of a bag. There was a low "ah" in the courtroom. He laid it on the table in front of Mom. I gave Nicky a little elbow and got a bigger one back.

"Please tell the court where you acquired this vest."

"From Lance McQuiddy's closet in his room in Independence."

"What did you find in examining this vest?"

"Well, it's made from the pop-tops of cans, mostly sodas. The loops are cut and linked together. But over here …" She turned the vest in her hands. "Here is a tear in the links, and several links are turned open with sharp edges exposed. This one …" She took hold of one of the links and held it up. "This one had blood matching Sheriff Matson's DNA on it."

"Sgt. McQuiddy, is there any of this blood on this shirt or this vest that could be linked to Terrence?"

"No, sir."

"Thank you, Sgt. McQuiddy." As Prosecutor Stamper sat down, he scowled at Sheriff Matson. I hated the Sheriff, too, but not as much as I hated my dad being a mental patient.

Chapter 24

NICKY

BY THIS POINT IN the trial, McQuiddy was a total basket case. Finding out his dad was alive was one thing. Finding out he was a patient in Independence Hospital was another. As kids we used to joke about someone going to Independence. Real cruel, crazy guy stuff. But finding out the sheriff fought with his dad to get his can crusher had McQuiddy's eyes bulging and his fists turning purple.

Prosecutor Stamper had called a witness I didn't recognize.

"You are a fingerprint analyst for the Scott County Sheriff's Department, is that correct?"

"Yes."

"Tell us whose prints the investigator found on the

driver's window of Terrence's car the day they found his body."

"Sheriff Matson's."

"Any other significant prints?"

"Just the deceased's."

"Thank you." Mr. Stamper sat.

Gander rose slowly, flicking a piece of debris from his lapel. "Do you have any way of telling exactly how long those prints were there?"

"Not exactly."

"Yes—or no."

"No."

"No further questions, your honor."

Gander turned away and turned back. "Wait a minute. Sir, did you also analyze the fingerprints on the murder weapon, the so-called can crusher with all of the victim's blood on it."

"I did."

"And what did you find?" Gander took another gander at the jury.

"One set of prints."

"And whose were those?"

"Lance McQuiddy's."

That brought a stir in the courtroom and a frown to the boy's face.

The judge called a recess, and we slipped out the back of the courtroom and found Daddy chatting with some suits who had frowns on their faces. He came over to us.

"You kids better prepare yourself for a firefight," Dad said to us. "Your mom, Henry, is likely to be fuming mad."

"Why?" McQuiddy asked. "She's got him. He's guilty. She should be celebrating."

"There is no way the sheriff is going to jail on that evidence. It's all circumstantial. Unless they can come up with some concrete evidence that ties the sheriff directly to the murder of Terrence, he walks."

"Didn't they find the sheriff's blood on Terrence?" McQuiddy started to sound like a lawyer.

"No. They found only brown stains on his shirt collar and face. Turned out to be tobacco. Terrence must've been smoking when he was struck."

"You're joking, right?" McQuiddy looked like he was getting ready to call my dad some names, like he had with Duke.

"No."

I grabbed McQuiddy's arm. "Calm down, boy."

"Right." McQuiddy closed his eyes and took a breath. "One question. Does tobacco juice carry DNA in it?"

"Oh, my left foot!" Dad got this stunned look on his face and ran into the courtroom. He bashed into Henry's mom coming out of the room. He grabbed her shoulders and leaned in close whispering to her.

CHAPTER 25

HENRY

DURING THE BREAK IN the trial, Prosecutor Stamper asked the judge for another day to investigate some new evidence. Mom made it clear that night that I was not to say one word about the trial. Not one word. Nicky and I weren't even allowed to hang out. I think both her dad and my mom were worried we'd open our big mouths and blow the case. The truth is, I was much more worried about Mr. Stamper blowing the case.

The next day, Nicky and I met at the marble steps leading up to the courtroom. Thunder announced the coming of a big storm. With a prosecution who might have missed one of the most important pieces of evidence, I worried how this would go. Probably get the whole tobacco thing thrown out. At least we'd get to see this travesty from the third row.

Now that Mom knew we were there, and with what I'd told Nicky's dad, we managed to nab seats right alongside Mr. Smithers.

There was an electric energy in the room from more than the building storm. The first courtroom lightning bolt came as a new witness was escorted in through the back doors.

"Your honor," Mr. Stamper stood. "I call as the next witness for the prosecution, Norman Matson."

"Objection!" For the first time cool, collected Gander, yelled. "We have received no word of this witness." He adjusted his tie trying to regain his composure.

"Your honor, we have attempted to notify the defense of this witness by phone, by mail, and by hand delivery, but he has not seen fit to accept any form of communication from us."

Gander looked at his fancy pen poised above his notes on his lap. "I have no idea what Mr. Stamper is talking about."

"Both attorneys will approach the bench."

Here it comes, I thought. *The part where the judge throws out anything that makes the sheriff look bad.* I watched a heated argument between the three of them ending with the judge yelling at both of them to get back to their seats.

The judge turned to the jury. "While it is apparently true that the defense received no word of an additional witness, the witness is a very logical choice for a proceeding like this and the defense will have as much time as needed for cross-examination. Mr. Stamper, call your next witness."

"Norman Matson."

He wore jeans that were cut off at the knees and sandals with bright green socks. His flannel shirt was a mixture of pinks and purples. A crop of curly, blond hair sat on a pale face with delicate features.

"Please state your name for the record," said the court clerk.

"Norman Matson."

The clerk swore him in.

"What is your relationship with the accused?" Mr. Stamper asked.

"He's my father."

"And …" Mr. Stamper paused to look at the jury.

"What is your relationship to the deceased?"

Norman turned away taking a couple of deep breaths.

"Please, answer the question," the judge ordered.

"He was my—my boyfriend."

"What do you mean by *boyfriend*?" Stamper asked.

"You, of all people, should know exactly what I mean, Michael. We loved each other."

The courtroom thundered with chatter.

Mr. Stamper's faced turned beet red.

The judge pounded his gavel. "Let's have it quiet in the courtroom. Or you will be escorted out."

Once the courtroom settled, Mr. Stamper had regained his composure, "When's the last time you spoke with your father?"

"Well, the last time I *spoke* to him was two years ago." Terrence made a point of making no eye contact with his dad, Sheriff Matson.

"And do you remember what you talked about?"

"I'll never forget."

"Tell us what you remember."

"My father, Sheriff Matson, said that if I ever associated with that Terrence again, the next time I saw him would be at his funeral."

"Anything else?"

"Yes. He said he would spit on his grave. And then he spat a gob of tobacco juice in front of my feet." Norman looked up at his dad with loathing in his eyes.

"When is the last time you talked to Terrence?"

"The day before my dad murdered him."

"Objection!"

"Sustained. Just answer the question."

"Did you in fact, talk to Terrence the day before his murder?" Mr. Stamper asked.

"Yes."

"And what did you talk about?"

"Now that his mom had passed, he said he was ready to move in with me here in Davenport."

"Where did you hold this conversation?"

"At the Busy Bea Café."

"And who was present at that café besides you and Terrence?" Prosecutor Stamper turned to the jury, watching their faces.

"My dad came in as we were going out."

"And what did you say to him? "

"Nothing. Like I said, the last time I spoke to him was two years ago."

"Did he say anything to you?"

"No."

"What did he do at that time?" Mr. Stamper glanced over at the sheriff but kept a calm face.

"He just sort of sniffed the air—like he smelled something bad. Never looked right at us. Then he spat a gob of chewing tobacco, right on Terrence's chartreuse tennis shoes. And walked away."

That brought another small rumble from the courtroom.

"No further questions, your honor." Mr. Stamper sat.

DA Gander was slower to his feet this time. He looked back and forth between Sheriff Matson and Norman Matson. "Son, do you love your dad?"

Norman smirked. "I despise that man."

"What man?"

He pointed at the sheriff with fire in eyes. "That—that—animal!"

Another rumble in the room.

"Your honor, I would like this boy declared a hostile witness. It's obvious his feelings for the defendant have tainted his testimony."

The judge took a long look at Norman. "Sustained."

Gander smoothed his feathers and sat.

"Any other witnesses, Mr. Stamper?" the judge asked.

"Thank you, your honor. We have one more witness. The prosecution calls Dr. Sheryl Anderson, forensic scientist for the Davenport Police."

After she was sworn in and the courtroom quieted, Michael Stamper had just two questions for her. "Dr. Anderson, can you describe in detail what you found on the victim's face and collar?"

"Yes. There were traces of chewing tobacco in his nostrils and throat as well as under his eyelids and a stain of the same tobacco on his collar."

"And were you able to determine the origin of this tobacco?"

"Yes. An analysis of the tobacco revealed the DNA belonged to Sheriff Matson."

"No further questions, your honor." Mr. Stamper sat down, watching the jury.

Gander flapped his wings as he jumped to his feet. "Can you tell from these stains *when* they might have ended up on the boy's body?"

"Approximately."

"And what does that mean?" Gander shrugged, looking

at the jury.

"The stains were less than 48 hours old."

"So this *tobacco event* could have happened a day before the murder. Is that true?"

The doctor paused. "Yes."

CHAPTER 26

NICKY

IN THE CLOSING ARGUMENTS, defense attorney Joseph Gander rose to his feet shaking his head back and forth. "How sad is it, when a peace officer, the man in charge of ensuring your peace …" He looked sternly at the jury. "… is charged for the crime he, himself discovered and brought forward into the light of justice. He didn't hide anything. He didn't ignore the unusual presence of a mental patient in town, a patient who carried a device that became a murder weapon. The sheriff didn't try to shove a murder under the carpet of blind justice regardless of who the victim was. He discovered a victim, investigated, did his job, kept the peace."

Gander turned away from the jury and walked toward

the prosecutor's side of the courtroom. He looked Mr. Stamper right in the eye.

"The prosecution would have you listen to the hostile testimony of an estranged son and accept that—as evidence? Tobacco? Really?"

Gander turned and strolled back to the jury, then walked back and forth in front of them pondering his own words. "Not fingerprints on the weapon. Not blood. Not real evidence. The only blood on the can crusher that bashed in Terrence's head was his own, and the only fingerprints on the handle were the fingerprints of Lance McQuiddy."

Gander pointed to the sheriff. "A peace officer, ladies and gentlemen, a man doing his best to keep the peace. What a shame!" He paused a long time shaking his head. "What a shame! Your honor, the defense rests."

The sheriff folded his arms across his big chest and smiled at the judge.

McQuiddy squeezed the arms of his seat until his knuckles turned white.

From what my dad had told me, it didn't look great for conviction although I thought it looked pretty clear that he did it. Boy, sometimes I just don't know how grown men are going to behave. Yes, I do—like little boys. For my money, McQuiddy was looking saner and more grown up than the grown-ups.

"Prosecution?" The judge adjusted his reading glasses like he was getting ready to read a good book because this trial had become a waste of his time.

Michael Stamper rose, walked over to the jury silently, looked them each in the eye, turned, and walked back like he was getting ready to sit back down. I thought, *Oh, great! He's giving up.*

But he didn't sit down. He crossed past his own seat and walked over and stood beside Sheriff Matson. He lightly placed his manicured hand on the sheriff's shoulder, turned to the jury, and asked, "What would cause a man to spit in the face of another?"

"If you don't remove your hand from my shoulder, you're about to find out, deviant!" Sheriff Matson's face puffed up and turned purple as a plum.

That lightning bolt hit the courtroom dead center—followed by yelling and chattering and the judge banging his gavel until the cows came home.

The verdict was not much of surprise. Second-degree murder. Life imprisonment.

What *was* a surprise was that a week after the trial, the *Davenport Times* revealed some blood evidence that had been thrown out due to improper procedures for which nobody seemed to have an explanation. In the trunk of the sheriff's car, there were traces of blood belonging to Terrence Ashton.

Chapter 27

HENRY

WITH THE SHERIFF GONE, the tension with Mom had ended. And now I knew where Mom had gone on those Saturdays.

"You know what, Mom?" I said over the Saturday morning pancakes. "There's really only one thing I need to know."

"What's that?" She was wearing that new dress she bought, with the little purple flowers. Her perfume changed from an almond smell to a sort of lilac.

"What happened to Dad?"

She closed her eyes like she was praying for a moment. I think she actually was. She opened her eyes.

"He's safe."

I just looked at her. I knew she knew that that wasn't even close to the answer I was looking for.

"He's still up at the Independence Hospital."

"You mean the Independence State Mental Hospital." I frowned at her.

"Yes. Henry, he's not coming back. He probably never should have left there. But I visit him. At first it was to get information he had on the murder case. But I've kept on. Once in a while I see a little glimpse of the man I love and married. That's where I'm headed now. Wanna come?"

I was floored! What really surprised me was how *not* mad at my mom I was for hiding all that from me. She started those visits about six weeks ago. And, as I sat there wrestling with her words, all I could think of was that she must really love my dad. I mean, *no matter what.*

I stood up, walked over, and put a hand on my mom's shoulder. "Not ready, Mom."

"Okay." She looked up at me with shiny eyes.

I gave her shoulder a squeeze as I gazed at the picture of Dad on the wall in his Army dress greens. In my mind, I saluted him.

CHAPTER 28

NICKY

YOU'D THINK AFTER THE trial that McQuiddy would return to acting like a human being, but no. He marched around the school like a robot soldier. Still ignoring everyone. Even though everyone knew that the marijuana had been planted in his locker by the sheriff.

But I mean, I had my own things to work out. Sure, McQuiddy's dad didn't murder Terrence. But he maybe caused my mom's death, and he for sure saved my life. How do I wrap my head around all that?

At least I don't go walking around school all zombie-like, like McQuiddy. Something turned inside the boy at that memorial. While he was saying goodbye to his dad, he said goodbye to all his emotions. Shut down. Replaced them with basketball. Basketballs don't feel.

Coach Ellsworth finally talked him into joining the team. The boy was quick and tall and could shoot the net right off the basket.

One Saturday we headed for Davenport Central High on a school bus. The Northeast Junior High boys' basketball team and girls' volleyball team. That was us. The East Iowa Junior High Basketball Tournament was in the main gym. The East Iowa Junior High Girls' Volleyball Tournament was in the girls' gym. Schools came all the way from Dubuque.

I swear the whole bus smelled like an old tennis shoe. Boys sat in the back, and we girls sat sideways in our seats in the front so we could check out which guys were checking *us* out. Made no sense whatsoever.

Coaches sat in the very front. I was pretty sure Coach E, as the basketball team called him, had a thing for our coach, the much younger, Miss Perkins. Consequently, supervision was at a minimum.

Blanche made her move. "Scooch closer to the window, Nicky, so I can invite Henry over."

I squeezed to the window, opening a third seat on the aisle.

Blanche had no shame. She leaned out into the middle of the aisle, her blond hair cascading around her perfect face, and looked back directly at the boy. "Henry, could you come here a minute, please?"

McQuiddy marched up the aisle, shoulders slumped like he was walking down death row or something.

All the guys had a ball:

"All right, McQuiddy!"

"Kissy, kissy!"

"Woooo!"

They were merciless.

By the time McQuiddy got to us, I swear, his face had gone from red to purple. "Hi." He glanced at both of us.

Blanche patted the seat beside her. "Hi, Henry."

He slouched down in the seat sticking one long leg out into the aisle. The boy still wore black canvas tennis shoes but now with black laces.

"Hey, Nicky."

"Hey, yourself." I think the boy was glad I was there.

Blanche served the first volley. "You starting today?"

"Nah," McQuiddy replied. "Sixth man."

"Not bad for a seventh grader," Blanche kept her blue eyes locked on McQuiddy's face, her blue eyes gazing at him like a cat stalking a mouse.

"Guess not." McQuiddy had no clue how to talk to a girl like Blanche. I had to bite my lip to keep from laughing.

Blanche, however, had no problem with that. "Well …" She served another volley. "Coach says you're a natural, says you'll be a star at Central someday."

"Oh?"

Then Blanche serves an ace. The boy never knew what hit him.

"Yeah—like your dad." With that, she slipped a smooth hand onto the boy's quivering arm. The girl had no shame.

McQuiddy turned to face Blanche's gorgeous blue eyes. His mouth gaped open halfway and his eyes pretty nearly crossed.

"His dad?" I had to ask on behalf of the boy. Paralysis had obviously set into his throat.

"He played for Davenport. A big star." Blanche smiled like a golden retriever with a bird in her mouth. I pictured McQuiddy with missing feathers. She had him by the throat. He still couldn't speak.

"Really, Henry. Daddy told me." She squeezed his arm.

Guess who *Daddy* was? You got it. Coach E, the married guy flirting with the volleyball coach.

For the first time, I had this funny feeling in me about the boy. I did *not* like Blanche's hand on his arm. I had this totally stupid and totally embarrassing thought. *That should be my hand.*

That's the very moment I stopped calling the boy *McQuiddy* and started calling him *Henry.*

***

I'll never forget that first time we walked into the Davenport Central High School Blue Devil Gymnasium. The floor shined so brightly it hurt your eyes, the same floor that Henry's dad played on. A bright, blue devil holding a pitchfork in the center jump circle warned rivals they were in for a fight.

Wood bleachers crowded to the edge of the court. Behind them on the second level, additional concrete seats disappeared into the shadows above. More seats than the population of McGrawsland. I imagined the roar of the crowd when Central scored.

Well, our number 46, McQuiddy, had a fantastic tournament on that court. Averaged fifteen points a game, ten rebounds, and five blocked shots. This from a boy who couldn't walk and scratch his nose at the same time.

Me, I had twenty-two kills in three volleyball matches,

but who's counting? Northeast Junior High ruled. Boys and girls.

After showers I waited for Blanche at the trophy case with my gym bag in hand. She always took an extra five minutes to fix her makeup to look like she was just naturally beautiful, which she already was.

I checked out the trophies. *Good golly, Miss Molly!* There it was, the team picture. The 1959 State Championship Runners-Up. In the back row, the tallest kid, with a flattop haircut, Lance McQuiddy. No doubt about it—grinning with that same look Henry gets when he's just caught a crappie bigger than mine. A lot of my boy in that face.

The boy's team exploded out of the locker room snorting like pigs in the mud. Henry remained quiet. Not one snort on his face. He pinned his basketball to his hip with an elbow. He must have been a little proud. Still wore his game jersey with his jeans. In one hand he gripped his gym bag and a little gold trophy for MVP.

"Henry." It sounded nice—using that name.

Henry shuffled over, probably expecting a pat on the back. More like a "nice game" from me. Instead, I gave him what must have felt like a kick in the knee. I stepped aside revealing the picture in the trophy case. "Look at this."

Henry froze. His eyes went immediately to the back row. His gym bag and trophy dropped to the concrete floor. His eyes locked on the blue eyes of the tall kid in the photo.

"Check it out." I pointed to the leather basketball below the picture. The signature right in the middle: *Lance McQuiddy*.

The boy's eyes shifted to the ball. Clenching his teeth, he nodded his head up and down.

I took hold of his elbow watching his face.

He put a hand on my arm. "It's okay, Nicky."

As his hazel eyes gleamed at me, something like lightning shot though me. I swear.

"It's time, Nicky."

"To see your dad?"

"Yeah."

He bounced his ball once real hard on the concrete floor. It echoed off the back wall of the Blue Devil gym. "Check out his number."

The number on his dad's jersey was 46.

CHAPTER 29

HENRY

THE NEXT SATURDAY MORNING my mom was up way before me. I found her dancing around the kitchen humming to herself.

"Those blueberries?" I asked.

"Yep, your dad's favorite."

"I'll take ten pancakes, please." My record was nine at one sitting.

"Sure."

Wait a minute. She agreed too quickly. "What are you up to, Mom?"

"Nothing. Oh. Well. I do have a little surprise, but I think you'll like it."

A knock came at our door.

Before the third knock hit the kitchen door, Mom had it open. "Come in, Nicky. We'll be ready in ten minutes. Want any pancakes?"

Now I really freaked out. The person my mom addressed as *Nicky*? She was wearing a dress! Well, a navy-blue pleated skirt and a light blue blouse with … I wiped my eyes … little orange flowers on it!

"No thanks, Mrs. McQuiddy. Full up on eggs and sausage." Nicky sat across the kitchen table from me. "Close your mouth, Henry. You'll catch flies."

It was her all right. I dived into my pancakes for comfort. Seven pancakes later, Nicky spoke.

"Did you tell him?" she asked Mom.

"Wha?" A mouthful of pancake muffled my question.

"I'm going with you—to Independence."

"Actually, Henry's not going anywhere dressed like that." Mom referred to my orange T-shirt and favorite patched blue jeans. "You go get yourself a nice dress shirt and clean jeans. And don't forget your jacket. There might be snow."

"Go." Mom gave my shoulder a little squeeze as she picked up my plate with three pancakes left on it. I smelled the faint suggestion of lavender perfume.

***

Mom tossed a bag of sandwiches on the dashboard of her El Camino as Nicky and I squeezed in together on the bench-style seat.

"Buckle up." Mom adjusted her rearview mirror and started the car.

Nicky grabbed the seat belt, pulled it across her waist, and handed it to me. I pulled it on past my waist and buckled it into the latch by my door. It was one good thing about being skinny. You could still buckle two with one belt. The other good thing about being skinny is that I could really leap. Not many junior high boys could slam-dunk a basketball. Just saying.

The problem now was, for the first time, I felt uncomfortable sitting next to Nicky. She'd gotten curves—girl curves.

With a four-hour ride ahead of us, Mom tried to make conversation. "You nervous about meeting your dad?"

"No."

"Really?"

"Met him before," I said.

That shut down talk for a half hour until Nicky floored

me with her question.

"Can I tell her about the river?" Nicky asked.

"What river?" Mom asked.

"Go ahead." As if I had a choice after that question.

Nicky told the whole story of Dad rescuing her in the Wapsi. And how I got her to shore with a branch.

"Still pulling people out of rivers." Mom referred to Dad's Bronze Star for carrying wounded platoon members across a Vietnam river during a firefight.

Both Nicky and Mom kept firing little questions at me like, "When did you know it was him?" and "What are you going to say?"

I answered them with two-word answers, mostly "don't know." I was done talking. I had too many questions of my own banging around in my head like, *What will my dad be like now?*

My brain felt scrambled. I just dunked all the other questions that swam around in there into a dark pool of mindlessness. I stared out at the cornfields whizzing by.

***

An enormous attendant pulled out a set of keys hanging from his belt and unlocked the first door, then the second door, which led us to the ward. He had to be like a former nose guard for some NFL team, long, blond strands of hair, a scruffy beard, and a full-toothed grin that looked more like he was ready to eat you than to greet you.

He held up a clipboard and read, "Nicky Smithers. Doris McQuiddy. Henry McQuiddy."

When he said my name, it felt like someone grabbed me around my neck. I couldn't breathe. The medicinal smell, the highly polished floors, and the pea-green stucco walls brought me a wave of nausea.

"I feel sick."

Mom took my arm. "It's okay, Henry. He's just down the hall. He's been asking how you are."

"We can do this." Nicky took my other arm.

"He's, he's here?"

"He's here, Henry, but not *all* here," Mom said.

"I—I'm not ready for this." I tried to pull away but both ladies had latched onto me.

"Sorry," Mom said. "You don't get to change your mind on this one. Too long a drive."

Nicky gently squeezed my arm.

The three of us stepped into a quiet room with a window facing some woods out back of the institution. A large man in a blue, pinstripe shirt, blue jeans, and slippers sat in a chair staring out at the trees.

I studied the man. *Was he Dad?* A recent haircut revealed a few gray streaks under a broad head of brown hair. His clean-shaven face tightened at the jaws. He clenched his teeth like I do. *Can he talk?* He turned. His blue eyes widened.

"Hello." I started trembling.

He nodded and reached for something in his shirt pocket.

I stared at his arms. The cuffs of his shirt folded back. Around his wrists, gray scar tissue. On his right arm, under a tattoo of the three interlocking hearts, the words read, *NO MATTER WHAT.* He pulled out the picture I had given him, pointing at the kid in the picture and nodding at me.

I studied his face. His eyes looked far away—somewhere real far away. But there were tiny moments. Like when he looked at the picture. Moments when he was present. My dad was in the room, somewhere.

"Do you know who this is?" I took Nicky's elbow.

He looked more than confused—scared, like he'd done something bad.

"This is Nicky, my best friend. You saved her life."

Nicky stepped forward. "Thank you, Mr. McQuiddy."

He shot a look of fear at Mom."

"It's okay, Lance," Mom said. "You didn't do anything wrong. None of us did anything wrong."

Mom's words pierced my heart like a lance. *You didn't do anything wrong, Dad. Really. You didn't do anything wrong. Neither did I.*

"Dad?" A lump throbbed in my throat.

He cast his blue eyes at me filled with questions. "Yes."

"How are you?"

He began rocking back and forth in his chair, holding his knees. "*RA54925348 … RA54925348 … RA54925348.*"

"He needs a rest, now." Mom gave him a warm smile.

Dad nodded in agreement.

I offered him my hand. "See you later."

To my shock, he took it in his huge, weathered hand. "Watch out for snags."

"Sure," I said. "I will, Dad."

His hand began to tremble. He gently pulled my hand toward him as he stood up. His arms came around me, big arms, man arms. And as new as this hug was to me, it felt strangely familiar. I wrapped my arms around my dad, and we held each other for several seconds. His hand came up to my shoulders, and he stepped back gazing into my eyes. "Bye, son."

"Bye, Dad." I felt such a mixture of feelings. Sad, sure. Really sad. But at the same time, strong—like nothing could stop me now. I knew my dad was always there for me—*no matter what.* And that hug, that one hug could get me through anything.

***

The powdery snow of the first winter storm swirled around the windshield wipers of Mom's El Camino on the drive home. We didn't talk for the first thirty miles. We all seemed lost in our own thoughts.

Mine were about my two riding companions. First, there was my mom. I mean my real mom. She was back. I glanced over at her. Her molasses eyes smiled, even though her forehead creased and her lips tightened. How had she managed to put up with me all these years, me and my smart mouth. She never gave up. *Even when Dad* … I stopped that thought, breaking the silence. "So. He's never coming home, is he?"

"Probably not." Mom put an arm around Nicky.

Most of Nicky's freckles had faded from her slightly upturned nose. Rust-colored eyelashes tried to blink back her feelings, but I could tell.

Here was this girl squished right beside me with her thigh pressed against mine. I thought she was still Nicky, my best friend. But I felt nervous around her for the first time, almost scared. It kind of hurt and felt nice at the same time.

Nicky set a personal best record for the longest time she ever went without saying a word. Pretty much the whole trip.

The Iowa winter slipped through the cracks in the door like icy fingers.

A few minutes later, much warmer fingers interlocked with mine. Nicky's smooth, strong hand gripped mine.

I looked over at her. Her head lay on Mom's shoulder. Mom pulled her closer. The faint gray glow of the Iowa winter glistened in the silent tears streaming down Nicky's face.

I squeezed her hand.

THE END

ACKNOWLEDGEMENTS

The people I would like to acknowledge all have the same thing in common. They have endured, fallen asleep to, or actually enjoyed my writing and my story-telling:

I must first mention my writer's group, The Ojai Scribes, with whom I have met weekly for over fifteen years. In particular, I'd like to thank the longest-standing members: Anne Boydston, LaNette Donoghue, and Pat Hartmann, as well as our newest member, Dena Hayess Horton.

Then there's my wife, Margaret, who often had to listen to a story-telling talk multiple times, sometimes even in the morning, before she'd had her coffee, and was always so supportive. My daughter, Lisa, was raised on Magic Pencil Girl stories. My son, Robert, took road trips with me to the tales of Gross Booger, the smelly superhero.

There are the, perhaps thousands of, Toastmasters who have heard my stories from the stage; I thank you for your tears and your laughter.

And finally, there is the "fallen asleep to" category. At between ages 8 and 12, I would tell made up stories to my younger brother and sister, back when we all slept in the same room, Chris and I in the bunk bed, Lynne around the corner in a single. I always finished the stories, whether they were awake or not.

Thanks readers! Thanks listeners!

Actually there is one more category of person I would like to acknowledge, the guy who gently but clearly gives me a nudge, when I fall asleep, to move on with my writing projects and move them to completion, John J. Hruby, my writing coach!

About Pat

As an educator for over 40 years, Patric Peake spent four years as an elementary principal, learning what stories lit up the eyes of 4th 5th and 6th grade readers. He gave each of his upper grade teachers a half hour of extra prep time by reading aloud to their students once a week. With two teachers at each grade level, he was reading every day. And mostly he read Newberry prize-winning books. He found out that girls loved hearing boy's books more than the reverse. However, he found that boys loved stories that brought out the emotions of the boy hero.

Pat has touched the lives of students from kindergarten to graduate level college. His wife, son and daughter have endured hundreds of stories he would tell them. It all started at age eight when he would tell nightly stories to his younger brother and sister when they all slept in the same room.

Now, he writes them.

Two books, “Magic Pencil Girl” and “Inspector Pepper” that Pat has written are available on his website:

http://patricpeake.com

Magic Pencil Girl

Listen to an audio book of a sixth grade girl who has lost her dad and is negotiating through a rocky time in elementary school with the assistance of her magic pencil. When she draws something with it, and taps the drawing with her eraser, it comes alive!

Inspector Pepper

Read murder mysteries that were designed originally for people with memory loss. Hence the subtitle: “From Crime to Cuffs in less than 10 minutes. This tongue-in-cheek crime series is just a fun read.